FREDDY
Rides AGAIN

The Complete FREDDY THE PIG Series
Available from The Overlook Press

Please inquire about special prices on a complete set (or sets) of the original twenty-six Freddy books at sales@overlookny.com

FREDDY
Rides
AGAIN

by WALTER R. BROOKS

With illustrations by
Kurt Wiese

THE OVERLOOK PRESS
New York, NY

If you enjoyed this book, very likely you will be interested not only in the other Freddy books published in this series, but also in joining the *Friends of Freddy*, an organization of Freddy devotees.

We will be pleased to hear from any reader about our "Freddy" publishing program. You can easily contact us by logging on to either THE OVERLOOK PRESS website or the Freddy website.

The website addresses are as follows:

THE OVERLOOK PRESS
www.overlookpress.com

FREDDY
www.friendsoffreddy.org

We look forward to hearing from you soon.

This edition first published in paperback in the United States in 2013 by

The Overlook Press, Peter Mayer Publishers, Inc.
141 Wooster Street
New York, NY 10012
www.overlookpress.com
For bulk and special sales, please contact sales@overlookny.com

Library of Congress Cataloging-in-Publication Data
Brooks, Walter R., 1886-1958
Freddy rides again / Walter R. Brooks : illustrated by Kurt Wiese
p. cm.

Manufactured in the United States of America
ISBN 978-1-4683-0724-5
2 4 6 8 10 9 7 5 3 1

FREDDY

RIDES AGAIN

Chapter 1

Jinx, the cat, was curled up in Mrs. Bean's rocking chair on the back porch of the farmhouse. Hanging over the arm of the chair was his gun belt, and over the other arm was a cowboy hat, cat size. For since the early summer when Freddy, the pig, had learned to ride horseback, the cowboy craze had hit the Bean farm in a big way. Even the mice who lived in the cigar box under the stove went about the house with little gun belts strapped about their middles. Mrs.

Bean had made the belts for them out of bits of material from her sewing basket and Mr. Bean had whittled out little wooden pistols. Any hiker, cutting across the Bean farm pastures, was likely to be stopped a dozen times by a shout of "Stick 'em up, stranger!" and the sudden appearance of a squirrel or a rabbit, armed, apparently, to the teeth.

Though Jinx was asleep, his whiskers twitched irritably every time the argument, which was going on around the corner of the house, got louder. Finally, he opened his eyes. "Oh, *gosh!*" he exclaimed, and then he jumped down, buckled on his belt, and went around to where Georgie, the little brown dog, and Bill, the goat, and Mrs. Wiggins, the cow, were sitting under the maple tree.

"Look," he said, "Why do you have to ruin a nice peaceful summer afternoon with all this hullabaloo? Why can't you do your hollering somewhere else?"

"Why can't you do your sleepng somewhere else?" Georgie asked, and Bill said, "Yeah, or else put up a little sign: 'Silence! Cat asleep!' How would we be supposed to know that your lordship was enjoying his noble slumbers?

We'd have been as quiet as mice."

"Oh, sure," said Jinx, "That shows how much you know if you think mice are quiet. You just try sleeping in the kitchen some night, with those four under the stove in their cigar box. Eeny snores and Cousin Augustus has nightmares, and Eek walks in his sleep. Walked over to where I was sleeping the other night and bit me in the ear. Said he dreamt it was a piece of cheese."

Georgie giggled, and Bill said, "Ha! Piece of cheese, hey? So Eek thinks our Jinx is a big piece of cheese! And I suppose you still believe he was really asleep?"

"What!" said Jinx. "You mean you think— Why, that little—"

"Oh, good land, cat," said Mrs. Wiggins, "can't you ever take a joke?"

"Not when I'm asleep, I can't. Not in the middle of the night. Oh, well . . ." He yawned and began washing his face. "What were you arguing about?" he asked.

"I thought we'd get around to that pretty soon," said Bill with a grin. "You're so afraid you're going to miss something, Jinx. Curiosity—"

"Yeah, I know, I know," Jinx interrupted with a weary sigh. "Curiosity killed the cat. I wonder how many million times I've heard that! As if cats were any more curious than other animals. I bet if all the goats curiosity has killed were laid end to end they'd reach from here to San Francisco."

"Well, what's so wrong about being curious anyway?" Mrs. Wiggins said. "I'm perfectly free to say I'm curious as all get-out. My land, all the great inventions were discovered by curious people. What's curiosity anyway but trying to find out something you don't know? That's what schools and colleges are for—to satisfy people's curiosity about things they don't know about. Gracious, that's all our argument was—trying to decide what kind of a dog Georgie is."

"I keep telling you—I'm part wolfhound," said Georgie.

"It must be an awful small part, then," said Jinx. He looked critically at Georgie. The dog was small, and everything about him was just sort of halfway—neither curly nor straight-haired, neither brown nor grey, with legs and ears neither long nor short. It is almost impossible to describe him; he was just a dog. But he had a very pleasant and friendly expression.

"I'm part wolfhound," Georgie repeated, "and part police dog, with just a little Siberian boarhound mixed in."

Jinx laughed. "Look, you dope," he said, "those are all big dogs. And you aren't much bigger than a rabbit. How could you be descended from them?"

"Lots of big people have little children," said Georgie. "Anyway, I'm not through growing yet."

"Well, one thing I'm sure of," said Mrs. Wiggins, "is that you're part beagle. It's the expression on your face. All beagles have it, kind of eager and anxious to please."

"Kind of sweet and foolish," said Jinx. "That's what I heard Mrs. Bean say about him once—Ouch!" he yelled. "You quit that, Georgie, or I'll claw you good." For the dog had turned and nipped him sharply in the leg.

"It's the wolfhound in me," said Georgie with a satisfied smile. Then he jumped up quickly. "Hey, look up in the pasture there."

They all looked. "For Pete's sake," said Bill. "That's the silliest performance I ever saw. What's he think he is—a kitten? Let's go see."

Jinx grinned. "See what I mean?" he said. "Curiosity killed the goat." But he followed the others across the barnyard.

Freddy, the pig, was apparently chasing something. He would crouch and pounce, then leap up and swat the air with his fore trotters—exactly like a kitten trying to catch a butterfly. Only of course a pig's performance was not nearly as graceful to watch as a kitten's, and the four animals, after looking on for a minute or two began to giggle and then to laugh outright.

When he heard them, Freddy stopped and came over to the fence, looking rather sheepish. "Cy says I'm too heavy, so I've gone on a diet," he said. "Grasshoppers. They say they make you thin." Cy was a pony. Freddy had bought him to keep him from being beaten by his former owner. In return, the pony had taught him to ride, and now it was a familiar sight to see Freddy, in cowboy clothes with holstered pistols at his thighs, cantering about the countryside.

"Yeah, I've heard of that diet," said Bill. "But you can't eat 'em if you can't catch 'em. So what good does all this toe-dancing do? You haven't caught one yet."

Freddy was apparently chasing something.

"I expect it's the exercise trying to catch them that makes you thin," said Mrs. Wiggins. "Not the grasshoppers."

"I did catch one," said Freddy. "But when it came to eating him . . . well, you know he looked up at me with such a pathetic expression on his little face—well, I couldn't. Those big mournful eyes—"

"Stop, stop!" said Jinx. "You're breaking my heart. You remind me of my Uncle Herbie. He used to cry so when he caught a mouse he could hardly swallow him. He—"

"That reminds me, Jinx," Mrs. Wiggins interrupted; "there was a tortoise-shell cat came to call here yesterday when you were out riding. His name's Arthur, and he belong to those folks that bought the farm west of here. City folks named Margarine. They just moved in. But he wants to quit 'em. Wanted to know if he could come live with us."

"Well, he's got a nerve," said the cat. "I hope you told him where he got off."

"I said Mr. Bean had a cat and I didn't think he wanted another. But I said you'd probably return his call. He was a real nice quiet-spoken cat."

"Well, I might drop in on him," said Jinx. "Just to make sure he doesn't get any big ideas, and understands who runs things around here."

"And just to satisfy your curiosity about this Magarine outfit, hey, Jinx?" said Bill.

"Well, what's the harm in that?" Jinx demanded. "They're city folks . . . got lots of money. They've rebuilt the house and they've got riding horses and servants and so on; I expect there'll be parties and all kinds of goings-on —sort of pep things up around here."

"My land, I hope not," said Mrs. Wiggins. "Parties! Singing and carrying on and whooping it up half the night, I suppose. It'll just spoil our nice quiet life."

"Hey! Look, coming in the gate!" said Bill. "That's one of 'em now."

They turned to look. A boy on horseback had ridden into the barnyard. He had on expensive looking riding breeches and boots, and his horse wasn't a Western pony, like Cy; he was a tall, beautifully groomed thoroughbred. Both boy and horse looked around contemptuously; evidently they didn't think much of the Bean farm.

"That's the Margarine boy," said Georgie. "Billy, his name is."

"Let's creep down and have a look at him," said Jinx.

After hesitating for a few minutes, the boy rode up to the back porch. Without dismounting, he rapped on the railing with his riding whip.

Mrs. Bean came to the door, "Good morning," she said pleasantly. "You're Mr. Margarine's boy, aren't you? Won't you come in? I've just made a batch of sugar cookies."

Billy didn't answer her. "Is this Beans'?" he asked.

Mrs. Bean was a small, plump, apple-cheeked woman with merry black eyes. But now she drew herself up, and she looked about six feet tall, and her eyes weren't merry any more. "I am Mrs. Bean," she said, "and I just invited you in. Is this the way you usually reply to an invitation?"

The boy's face got red. "An invitation?" he said. "Oh, you mean asking me to come in. Yeah. Well, I didn't want to come in; I just wanted to see the talking animals I heard you had here."

Freddy and his friends had come up close to the porch. Bill whispered in Jinx's ear: "If this guy's name is Billy, I'm going to change my name to something else."

"Guess we're going to have to teach him some manners," Jinx muttered.

Mrs. Bean waved her hand towards them. "These are some of the animals," she said. "Whether they'll talk to you or not is another matter. And now if you'll excuse me—" She put her hand on the doorknob, but stopped as the boy, who had turned to look at the animals, suddenly burst into a loud laugh. "Oh, golly!" he exclaimed, pointing to Freddy. "What is *that*?"

"That is Freddy, our pig," she said. "What's the matter with you, boy? Haven't you ever seen a pig before?"

Billy stopped laughing long enough to say that he had seen pictures of pigs, but never a live one before. "I didn't know what funny looking animals they really were," he said. "Oh, *golly,* he's funny!" And he stared at Freddy and went off into another gale of laughter.

The animals were pretty mad. They often kidded and made fun of one another, but for a stranger to laugh at one of them was something different. But they were undecided just what to do. Although as animals who could talk they were famous through all that part of the state, they had long ago decided that it was better not to talk before strangers unless there was some good reason for it. And they didn't want to give the boy the satisfaction of hearing them.

Mrs. Bean knew that they were trying to make up their minds what to do to Billy, and instead of going in, she came to the edge of the porch. "You're a very rude boy," she said. "But I don't want to see you get hurt, and so I advise you to stop that laughing and ride on about your business."

"Pooh," said the boy. "You think I'm afraid of *them*?" And he laughed all the harder. And Mrs. Bean shrugged her shoulders and went into the house.

I don't know what the animals would have done, but the matter was taken out of their hands. For another friend of Freddy's had been watching. He was a wasp named Jacob and he was sitting on the porch railing in the sunshine polishing his sting. Wasps are pretty quick tempered, and when the boy began laughing he buzzed angrily, and as the laughter continued, he tested the point of his sting on the wood, and then he rose in the air, circled twice, and dove with an angry whine onto the neck of Billy's horse and jabbed the sting in up to the hilt.

The horse gave a snort and went straight up in the air, and Billy slipped sideways and lost his stirrups and grabbed the mane to keep from falling. And then the horse gathered his legs under him and bolted. They went up through the barnyard and sailed over the fence, and through the pasture, and as the animals watched, they disappeared among the trees of the Bean woods.

Jacob circled down and settled on Freddy's nose. "Well, I guess we settled that pair, hey, Freddy? Gave 'em a dose of old Dr. Jacob's soothing syrup."

"Thanks, Jacob," said the pig. "Only, you stung the wrong party. The horse didn't do anything."

"Anybody comes in our yard looking around as disgusted as that horse did," said the wasp, "gets the same medicine. Anyway, if I'd just stung the boy, he'd have yelled, and you know Mrs. Bean—she'd have gone all sympathetic and come out and given him cookies and milk. As it is, we gave 'em both something to laugh at, and got rid of 'em into the bargain."

"Well, I know one thing," said Mrs. Wiggins. "If that boy is going to be a neighbor of ours, we're going to have trouble."

"I think I'll go over and have a talk with that cat, Arthur," said Jinx. "It's a good time now, while the boy's away. And maybe we can get a line on these people. Want to go along, Freddy?"

Chapter 2

A little while ago the Margarine place had been just an old run-down farmhouse. Then Mr. Elihu Margarine had bought it, and he had brought in gangs of carpenters and masons and electricians and plumbers, and it was now as fine a mansion as you would find anywhere between Albany and Buffalo. Even the estate of their friend, Mr. Camphor, Jinx and Freddy agreed, wasn't as elegant.

The gateway alone was enough to scare off any real timid visitor. There were two huge stone gateposts, and on each was a frowning stone lion, holding in his paws the Margarine coat of arms. For the Margarines were a very old and aristocratic family. Their fortunes had first been founded by Phillippe de Margarine, who came to England (some say as a cook) in the train of William the Conqueror. The ancestor in whom Mr. Margarine took most pride was Sir Henry Margarine, who in one year, 1572, fought twenty duels, of whch twelve were wins and eight draws. Mr. Margarine himself did not of course fight duels: he was a banker. But he felt sure that he could be successful at dueling if he ever found time to take it up as a hobby.

The two friends went through the tall iron gates, then ducked off into the shrubbery and worked their way around to the back of the house. There was a man washing a big car, and two other men leading horses up and down. They stayed under cover and watched. After a while a tortoise-shell cat came out of the stable. He was large and sleek and had a very kindly and benevolent expression.

"Pssst!" said Jinx, and the cat came over to them.

Jinx introduced himself and Freddy, and the cat expressed himself as highly honored by the call. "I'm sorry I can't offer you any refreshment," he said. "But the truth is that Mrs. Margarine has given orders that I'm not to have anything to eat. That's why I came to see you yesterday—I thought maybe—if I could stay at your farm while I was looking around for another situation . . ."

"Why won't they feed you?" Jinx interrupted. "You been clawing the furniture or something?"

"Nothing like that," Arthur said. "No, my trouble is a tender heart. I was engaged here as a mouser, but mice are such cute little things . . . and good gracious, they have fathers and mothers just like everybody else, even though smaller. How anybody can bear to kill them I simply cannot see." And the tears came to his eyes just at the thought.

Jinx looked at Freddy. "You and the grasshoppers," he said.

"Sure," said the pig. "Your Uncle Herbie, too."

"Uncle Herbie cried over 'em, but he ate 'em just the same," said Jinx. "Sometimes he sobbed so hard he couldn't swallow, and sometimes he swallowed so fast he couldn't sob. But he managed to feel noble and at the same time get three square meals a day." He turned to Arthur. "Why don't you make a deal with the mice? Have 'em keep out of sight in exchange for your letting them alone?"

"If I'd done that in the beginning it would be all right," said the cat. "But it won't work because they know now that I won't hurt them no matter what they do."

"Well," Freddy said, "your tender heart does you credit. I guess we could stake you to a meal or two. But as to staying on—that's up to Mrs. Bean. Cats are in Mrs. Bean's department. You'll have to talk to her, eh, Jinx?"

The cat agreed rather grudgingly, and then Arthur thanked them. "I'd show you around the place," he said, "but these Margarine folks aren't very friendly. They'd probably tell the servants to chase you away."

"Yeah, we met the boy a little while ago," said Jinx, and told Arthur about it.

"Billy's a spoiled brat," Arthur said. "They

And tears came into his eyes just as he thought.

buy him everything he asks for, and let him do whatever he wants. He has plenty of pocket money, so he thinks he doesn't need to have any manners. You're going to have trouble with him, because his folks always back him up."

"Do you suppose he really hadn't ever seen a pig before?" Freddy asked.

"Sure he's seen pigs," said Arthur. "He was being rude on purpose. He's heard about you being famous as a detective, and laughing at *you* made *him* feel more important. You always feel superior to people you laugh at."

They went home the back way, across lots, and Arthur told them more about the Margarines. "They're crazy about fox-hunting," he said. "And that's one thing I think you're going to have trouble with 'em about."

"Oh, I don't believe so," said Freddy. "There's only one fox around here—a friend of ours, John— and I guess he can keep out of their way."

"I wasn't worried about the foxes," said the cat, "and when I said 'fox-hunting,' I didn't mean trapping them, or going out after them with a gun. What these people mean by fox-hunting is going out on horseback and running foxes down with a pack of foxhounds. And they have special clothes for it, just as cowboys have special clothes for being cowboys—red coats, usually. They even have special yells that they yell—'Yoicks!' is one of them. If you're a cowboy you yell 'Yippee!' and if you're a fox-hunter you yell 'Yoicks!' Pretty silly business, both of them."

"I don't agree," said Freddy stiffly. "I see nothing silly about 'Yippee!' or about the cowboy costume."

"You put your foot in it, mister," said Jinx. "Freddy here is the head cowboy on this range. And don't try to be funny about it, because he's powerful quick on the draw."

Arthur apologized. "I really don't know anything about cowboys," he said. "It's a bad habit of mine, to make fun of things I don't know anything about."

"Oh, I guess we all do that," Freddy said. "It's easier than to admit we're ignorant. But about this fox-hunting—I'm still not worried about John. He's smart enough to fool a pack of hounds."

"Maybe he is. But he's not smart enough to keep these hunters from riding through your fields and trampling the hay down."

"They won't do it more than once," said Jinx. "Not if Mr. Bean sees them. They'll be too busy picking birdshot out of their hides."

"Oh, Mr. Margarine will offer to pay for the hay he's knocked down. But if your Mr. Bean starts any shooting—Well, we'll wait and see."

When they reached the farmhouse, Jinx mewed at the back door until Mrs. Bean opened it. Then he and Arthur walked in.

"Good gracious me!" said Mrs. Bean. "Who is this? You can't bring strange cats into my kitchen, Jinx."

"He's Margarines' cat," said Jinx. "Or was. They won't feed him, so I said maybe you'd let him stay here a few days."

"Well, he can have something to eat here," she said. "But he can't come into the house. Good grief, how do you think the mice would like that?"

"Oh, ma'am, I wouldn't lift a paw against your mice," said Arthur earnestly. "To tell you the truth—I suppose it's very weak and un-cat-like of me but I never catch mice. Why, I look at it from the mice's point of view: how would *I* like being chased and eaten up by animals ten times my size? No, ma'am; I've got a very sympathetic nature; why, some of my best friends are mice."

The mice, under the stove, had been very quiet. To have a strange cat come into the kitchen was what it would be like for you or me to have a thirty-foot alligator push open our bedroom door. But realizing that both Mrs. Bean and Jinx were there to protect them, they became bolder. And Eek came right out on to the floor and said: "Aw, lay off that brotherly love stuff, cat. You're not fooling anybody."

Arthur shook his head sadly. "It's natural that you should feel that way, mouse," he said. "But I have no wish to intrude where I am not trusted." He turned to Mrs. Bean and Jinx. "Madam and cat," he said, "I thank you for your kindness. And now I will go."

"Where are you going?" Jinx asked. "Back to the Margarines'?"

"No! No! For I would rather starve than to earn my keep by persecuting my little fellow animals. No, I shall take to the road. Perhaps somewhere I may find some kind person who will trust me and take me in."

"Oh, my goodness; what's all the fuss about?"

Mrs. Bean said. "I didn't say you couldn't stay here; I just said you couldn't stay in the kitchen. Plenty of space to sleep in the barn. Go out on the porch and I'll get you some milk."

As she opened the door for them, Eeny said: "So we're stuck with a cannibal around the place now, hey? What are we going to do?"

"Nothing, now," said Quik. "I wish Mrs. Bean wasn't so easily taken in by good manners and a pleasant smile. Anybody that knows anything about cats ought to know better than to trust one that wears as saintly as expression as that Arthur."

"That's right," Cousin Augustus said. "I always remember what my Aunt Minnie said about cats. 'Never trust a cat that has a saintly expression,' she said. 'Because no cat is saintly, and if he looks that way, it means he's putting on an act. And that act is probably going to end up with you inside him.' Poor Aunt Minnie! She was awful smart about cats, but she outsmarted herself in the end. Tried to talk a cat out of eating Uncle Wilfred; she did and he ate her instead."

The other mice had heard this sad story many times, so they just said: "Yeah. Too bad," and went on talking over what they could do about Arthur.

But during the next few days they began to think that they had no cause for worry. Arthur was certainly a perfect gentleman. He set up housekeeping in the box stall in the stable where Hank, the old white horse, lived. He was most polite to all the animals, and never even chased the chipmunks who called him names, or the red squirrels who threw things at him when he walked under the trees where they lived. After a day or two he invited the mice to call, sending the invitation by Jinx.

"Will you be there, Jinx?" Eek asked.

The cat grinned. "Boy, will I!" he exclaimed. "Quite a party, I understand. And first class refreshments! He's ordered 'em already."

"Ordered refreshments?" Quik asked. "I didn't hear anything about that."

"Sure you did," said Jinx. "He invited you four mice, didn't he? Two for him and two for me."

"Aw, quit trying to be funny, cat," said Eek. "Tell us what you think, will you? Do you think we should go call on this Arthur?"

Jinx looked sober and shook his head. "This

Arthur," he said. "He may be O K. I don't know. But any mouse that goes to a cat party is out of his mind, if you ask me. No, if the guy wants company, let him ask someone his size."

So the mice sent regrets.

Chapter 3

It was six in the morning when several heavy
thumps on the pig pen door woke Freddy up.
He opened one eye, said sleepily, "Oh, go
away!" then burrowed down and pulled the
covers over his head.

But the thumps continued.

"Oh . . . my . . . *goodness!*" he growled
angrily, and got up and threw the door open.
Cy, his buckskin pony, was standing outside.

"Boots and saddles, pig; boots and saddles!"

Cy shouted and then began singing: "A-hunting we will go! A-hunting we will go! . . ."

"Oh, shut up, will you?" said Freddy crossly. "What on earth's the matter with you, waking me up in the middle of the night? I'm not going a-hunting or anywhere else until I've had my breakfast."

"That's what *you* think," said Cy. "Look, Freddy; these new neighbors we've got, these Margarines, they're out on horseback with four foxhounds. Personally, I haven't any feeling about foxes, one way or another. But this John —he's a friend of yours—"

"John?" Freddy exclaimed. "You don't mean—?"

"No, they aren't hunting John, as far as I know. But if they run on to him—well, what chance would one fox have against four hounds?"

"O K," said Freddy, "be right with you," and dashed inside. A couple of minutes later he came out, lugging his saddle. He had on his cowboy costume—jeans, boots, thunder-and-lightning shirt, gun belt and ten gallon hat,— and with the two guns in his holsters, he looked like a pretty dangerous character. Of course, one of the guns was loaded with blanks, and the other was just a water pistol, but they had been more than a match for at least one fully armed Westerner, Cal Flint, whom the animals had driven out of the county a month or two ago.

John had been spending the summer, as usual, in a hollow tree on the Bean farm; but with the approach of fall he had moved up into a den on the edge of the woods. He was at home and came out when Freddy knocked.

"I thought I heard those hounds this morning," he said, when Freddy had told him about the hunters. "I scouted around the Margarine place the other night. Quite a joint. Found a big bowl of milk by the back door. Guess they must have known I was going to call, eh?" He laughed. "But pshaw, Freddy, you don't need to worry about me, though it's nice that you do. But if I can't fool a pack of silly hounds, I deserve to get chewed up. Which way did they go? I think I'll go over and give 'em a little fun."

Cy said: "That robin friend of yours, J. J. Pomeroy—is that his name?—he says they rode up north and then swung east around the Big Woods on to Mr. Witherspoon's farm. He's flown up to keep an eye on 'em." He pricked up his ears. "Hey, somebody coming. Maybe one of the hunters."

John's ears had gone up too. " 'Tisn't a horse," he said. "Not heavy enough. They waited and presently they saw the newcomer, moving slowly up along the edge of the woods.

It was Bill, the goat, and astride him, on a saddle made of some old burlap bags tied around him wih rope, sat Jinx, in his cat-size cowboy hat, and with his gun belt strapped around his middle.

"Well, will you look at that!" said Freddy with a grin. "He said he was going to get him a horse, but I didn't believe him."

"Hi, pardner," John called. "If you come in, come in a-shootin'."

Jinx rode in towards them. "Hi, fox," he said. "Oh, hello, Freddy. Have you warned John about the hunters?"

"He doesn't want to be warned," Freddy said. "He wants to go play with the hounds."

"Say, look, dope," Jinx addressed himself to the fox. "These aren't just any old dogs . . . they're *foxhounds*. When they chase you, boy! you *stay* chased until they catch you. But who am I to argue with a dunderhead? Go on up and get your ears chewed off. See if I care!"

But John just grinned at them. "Don't you worry about me. I'll fix these Margarines. I should think you'd be glad to get the laugh on them. You specially, Freddy. After the way that boy was laughing at you yesterday."

"Oh, I didn't mind that," Freddy said. "Maybe he really hadn't ever seen a pig before. Why I suppose if you and I had never seen a boy before, we'd laugh ourselves sick the first time we saw one."

"Yeah," said John, "or a cat."

"Hoh!" said Jinx contemptuously. "If there's anything funnier than a fox, dragging a tail around that's bigger than he is—"

"What are you going to do, John?" Freddy asked. "Follow me and see," the fox said. "But don't get too close. Maybe you'd better ride along with the hunters. Come on."

He went out between the trees. Once in the open he began to run. He didn't run as a dog does, high on his legs; he seemed to flow along the ground, almost like a snake. He went over a wall, up through the Bean pastures, and then over another wall on to Mr. Witherspoon's farm. And there ahead of them, moving along beside a fence, they saw the hunters—five of them on tall sleek horses, and with them four black and white spotted hounds.

Jinx and Freddy rode up towards them, while John made a circle and ran down close to them, but on the other side of the fence. There he kept moving around until the hounds saw him and came over to investigate. And then as they began excitedly baying and climbed the fence, he set off at full speed across the field.

And the riders followed. They backed off to get a good start, and then put their horses at the fence and sailed gracefully over. "Yippee!" Freddy yelled. "Go on, Cy!" But the pony didn't move.

"Look, pig," he said, "I'm no jumper. I don't say I couldn't make that fence, if you weren't on my back. But you're thirty pounds overweight. You lift down that top rail and then climb over; I'll join you on the other side."

So Freddy dismounted. While he was taking down the rail, Bill, with Jinx on his back, went over the fence a little farther down. Bill didn't really jump it; he jumped to the top rail, changed feet and down on the other side. Fred-

dy was a hundred yards behind when they went
on.

The chase swept on, over fields of stubble
where corn and hay had been cut, over walls
and fences, up a long low hill, then down and
across a wide valley and up another hill. Jinx
was **not** far behind the hunters, but Freddy kept
falling farther and farther back; Cy could jump
low walls and ditches, but he said he wasn't going to get tangled up with any wire fences, so
in several places they had to go a long way
around to get from one field to the next.

John may have noticed this; at any rate he
doubled back, just when they came within
sight of Otesaraga Lake; and the entire hunt
came pouring down on Freddy. The fox grinned
at the pig as he flashed past. "See you at Witherspoon's," he said. Then the hounds streamed
by, and Freddy reined Cy around to ride along
with the hunters.

But one of the men cut at Cy with his whip.
He was a small man with thin lips and hard
eyes, and Freddy knew he was Mr. Margarine.
"Get out of here!" he said. "Go on—beat it!"
And Freddy pulled back.

"Say, what's the matter with you!" said Cy disgustedly. "What you got those guns for? If you'd fired a blank that nervous thoroughbred of his would have turned a cartwheel and spread him all over the scenery."

"Sure, sure," Freddy said. "But I want to see what John is up to. You heard what he said. We'll take a short cut.—Hey, Jinx!" he called, as Bill and the cat came up. "John's making for Witherspoon's. Come this way."

So while John led the hounds and hunters by a roundabout route, they rode back to Witherspoon's by the road and so they got there first and saw the whole thing.

Mrs. Witherspoon was sitting on her back porch peeling potatoes. Back of her was the open kitchen window. There was no screen on the window, because Mr. Witherspoon was too stingy to buy a screen for her. Folks said that he wouldn't have bought a window for her to look out if there hadn't been one there when he got the house. She looked up and nodded when Freddy and Jinx rode through the yard. "Mr. Witherspoon's in the barn," she said, and went on peeling.

They raised their hats to her and rode on towards the barn, but they didn't go in. They pulled up behind some bushes where they could see without being seen. The voices of the hounds were coming nearer. They sounded like bells tolling. And then the hunt swept over the hill and down towards the house.

"Boy, can that fox run!" said Freddy admiringly. John streaked down and slipped through the fence that surrounded the barnyard, not more than a stone's throw ahead of the hounds, who scrambled through after him. The riders checked, then turned aside to find a gate. But John made straight for the house. He made one bound to the edge of the porch, a second to the arm of Mrs. Witherspoon's chair, and a third straight through the kitchen window.

Everything had happened so fast that Mrs. Witherspoon hadn't had time to jump up. She gave a thin scream as John brushed past her, and then the hounds, baying excitedly, crowded after the fox and piled all over her as they scrambled through the window. The chair went over, and for a minute the air was full of hounds and potatoes and Mrs. Witherspoon's frantic yells. And then suddenly everything was quiet again, with Mrs. Witherspoon lying on the

porch floor and a few potatoes rolling slowly
away from the overturned chair.

Mr. Witherspoon came hustling out of the
barn door, "What's going on here?" he shouted,
and ran up to the porch just as Mrs. Witherspoon got to her feet.

"Land sakes, Zenas, you must be deaf," she
said. "Didn't you hear me calling for help? You
better get those dogs out of the house."

But he didn't pay any attention to her, for
he had caught sight of one of the potatoes, which
was rolling to the edge of the porch. He grabbed
it just as it dropped to the ground. "Consarn it,
woman," he said angrily, "ain't you got anything to do but throw these good potatoes
around? You might at least pick 'em up."

She seized his arm and shook it. "The dogs,
Zenas! The dogs!" she shouted. "Listen!" And
she pointed to the window, from which came a
mixture of barks and yelps, and an occasional
crash, as some piece of furniture went over.

"Dogs!" he exclaimed. "How'd they get in
there? You let 'em in?"

"Chasing a fox," she said. "He went through
the window."

"I'll get a pitchfork," he said. But as he

The air was full of hounds and potatoes.

turned to go back to the barn, the huntsmen rode up.

"I'll get the hounds out for you," said Mr. Margarine, dismounting. "Sorry for this, but I'll make good any damage."

"Who are you?" Mr. Witherspoon demanded. And as Mr. Margarine came up the steps: "You keep out of there. I'll tend to this." He dashed off to the barn, but paused a moment to shout back to his wife: "You pick up those potatoes!"

"If they're your dogs, mister," said Mrs. Witherspoon, "you get 'em out of there quick." And Mr. Margarine went in the door.

"I hope they didn't catch John," Jinx said.

"You leave it to John," said Freddy. "A fox never lets himself get cornered."

"Hey, look," said Bill. "Here comes Old Man Trouble himself."

Mr. Witherspoon came out of the barn with a double-barreled shotgun in the crook of his arm. Mr. Margarine was still inside; Billy and Mrs. Margarine and their two friends had reined their horses up close to the porch and sat there looking on. None of them offered to help Mrs. Witherspoon pick up the potatoes.

Mr. Witherspoon pointed the gun at them. "Get out of my yard," he said.

"Oh, come, my good man," said Mrs. Margarine. "We're very sorry about this, but we'll pay for any damage our hounds may have done."

"You bet you'll pay, and plenty!" he said. "Sickin' your dogs on my wife!—Get that one!" he said to Mrs. Witherspoon, pointing to a potato which had rolled into a corner of the porch.

Mrs. Margarine laughed. "Don't be ridiculous!" she said. "The hounds went through the window after a fox."

Mr. Witherspoon gave a contemptuous snort. "Likely story!" he said. "You'd better think up a better one before you tell the judge about it. Foxes jumpin' through windows! I'm too old to listen to bedtime stories. Now git—all of you!"

The row in the house had quieted down, and as Mr. Witherspoon again lifted his gun menacingly, Mr. Margarine came out of the kitchen door, dragging the four hounds after him. He had snapped leashes on their collars, and though they yelped and struggled, he pulled them off

the porch. "Get down, Billy!" he said, "and
take Belle and Caroline. I'll take the other two.
The fox must be in there yet; we'll have to keep
them on leash or they'll go back in."

"Stand away from them dogs," said Mr. Witherspoon, and his gun swung to cover them.

Perhaps he didn't really intend to shoot them,
but Billy didn't wait to see. He brought his
whip down sharply on Mr. Witherspoon's wrist.
The man yelled and dropped the gun, and Billy
slipped quickly from the saddle and picked it
up. "O K, Dad," he said. "Let's go. I've got
him covered."

But Mr. Margarine handed the boy the
leashes and took the gun from him. He un-
loaded it and leaned it against the porch. "I'm
sorry about this," he said. "You know who I
am, I guess—Elihu Margarine. You send me the
bill for whatever damage has been done. Here's
fifty dollars to go on." And he held out a bill.

Mr. Witherspoon took it, looked at both sides
of it, then folded it and tucked it in his pocket.
He looked a little bewildered. After a minute
he turned and without a word stumped off towards the barn.

Freddy and Jinx watched until the hunters

had gone, and Mrs. Witherspoon had taken her potatoes back into the kitchen. Then they rode out and started home.

"That Margarine kid isn't a coward, anyway," said Bill.

"Oh, dear," said Freddy. "I was just getting so I hated him, and then he has to go do something I admire him for. I wish people would be good all over or bad all over. Even that Cal Flint we had so much trouble with this summer —you couldn't hate him as much as you wanted to, because there were some nice things about him. All the people we've had trouble with— Mr. Doty—even that old rat, Simon—they all had good things about 'em. And then you couldn't be as mean to 'em as you wanted to be."

"Oh, no?" said Jinx. "Well, I can. You just let me get a couple of claws in a good tender spot on that boy—" He broke off. "Hey, look!"

John was coming towards them along the top of a wall.

"How'd you get out here?" Freddy asked. "I thought you were in the house."

"Let 'em corner me there? Not me," said the fox. "When I jumped in the window, I just stood there close to the wall while the hounds jumped over me and began pulling the place to pieces. Then I jumped out while Mrs. W. was juggling those potatoes and sneaked off the side of the porch."

"I never took my eyes off the porch, and I didn't see you," said Cy.

"You weren't looking for me," said John. "You were watching the window, or Mrs. Witherspoon. If you'd expected me to come out, you'd have seen me."

"I guess that's so," said Freddy. "When I was a magician, I always had to get people's attention on something that didn't matter, so they wouldn't notice what I was really up to. But John, you took an awful chance."

"Pooh!" said the fox. "I want to get those hunters good and unpopular with the farmers around here, so that they'll have to quit this fox-hunting stuff. Anything for a quiet life. And you bet they won't ride across old Witherspoon's land any more."

"Maybe we could make a deal with the hounds," said Freddy, "not to bother you."

But John shook his head. "You can't argue with foxhounds, not on the subject of foxes.

They've got a single-track mind. Nice enough folks, I guess—kind to their families and so on. But they've been trained to chase foxes, and it's the one thing they just can't help doing. Just as Bill here can't help butting folks if he sees 'em leaning over. Just as you, Freddy, can't help—well—"

"Stuffing himself," put in Cy.

"Come on, Jinx," said Freddy, "I'll race you home."

Chapter 4

Arthur, the Magarine's ex-cat—as he sometimes referred to himself—was well liked by most of the Bean animals. He had a pleasing personality, and was much in demand at parties because of his genteel appearance and behavior. He was invariably polite, particularly to the more elderly animals, and was often invited to their homes.

Among the homes where he was a frequent caller was the little house up by the pond, where Alice and Emma, the two white ducks, lived with their Uncle Wesley. Emma, the more timid of the sisters, was still a little afraid of Arthur, but they were both impressed by the elegance of his manners, and pompous Uncle Wesley was completely sold on the handsome visitor.

Jinx disapproved of this friendship. He was very fond of the sisters, though as for Uncle Wesley, he said he didn't see why they gave him house room. "Just a bag of wind surrounded with feathers," he said to Freddy, "floating around with the rest of the scum on the pond. But the girls think he's wonderful. So when Arthur says he's wonderful too, they begin to think Arthur's pretty wonderful. Goes right around in a circle. Because Arthur sure thinks *they* are wonderful—or would be if he could have 'em for supper. A nice plump duck— mm *m'm!*" He smacked his lips.

"Oh, I don't think Arthur's up to anything like that," said Freddy.

"Yeah? Well, maybe not," said Jinx. "But— ever see the way he looks at 'em? Or at those rabbits he's always being so thoughtful of?— taking 'em little bouquets of lettuce and such. It ain't the way to look at a friend, Freddy; it's the way Mr. Bean looks at the roast turkey when he tucks the napkin under his chin on Thanksgiving."

The two friends were out riding together. They rode nearly every day, after Jinx had persuaded Bill that he would make a good cow pony. Bill had been easy to persuade, for a goat can gallop over broken ground where a horse would have to pick his way with great care, and can climb where a horse couldn't possibly follow. And Jinx of course needed neither saddle nor stirrups; he could hook his claws into the burlap sacks strapped to Bill's back, and nothing could shake him loose. It was quite a sight to see Jinx, waving his hat and yelling "Yippee!" as he rode Bill at a gallop along the top of a rough stone wall.

"Maybe we'd better speak to the ducks about Arthur," Freddy said, and they turned their horse's heads (or rather, one horse's head and one goat's head) towards the pond.

Alice and Emma were doing their powder-puff act, floating around on the water, and Uncle Wesley was sitting on the bank in the shade of a burdock leaf, grumbling as usual about the weather. There was nothing wrong with the weather, but it was always there and so saved him the trouble of thinking up something else to grumble about.

Freddy and Jinx dismounted, and then the horses and their riders all sat down on the bank as Alice and Emma swam towards them. Uncle Wesley went right on grumbling.

"Hi, girls," said Jinx breezily. "Seen any good shows lately?"

The ducks tittered. They liked Jinx, because he always pretended that they were very bold and dashing characters, out every night at a party or a dance.

"Well, maybe I'm speaking out of turn," said the cat, with a glance at the burdock leaf from under which came Uncle Wesley's discontented quacks. "But who was that duck I saw you with down at the movies the other night?"

Most of the farm animals did go down to the movies in Centerboro occasionally. Mr. Muszkiski, who managed the theatre, made a special low price for them, as he felt that animals, particularly such famous ones as Mr. Bean's animals, in the audience, were an added attraction. But the ducks never went.

"You didn't see us, Jinx," said Alice.

"Strange," said the cat. "I could have sworn it was you. With a handsome young duck I'd never seen before. Dark-complected fellow, with a very high polish on his bill. I'd say he waxed it."

Emma said: "We don't approve of the cinema, Jinx."

"You mean that old crab, Wesley, doesn't," said Jinx. "What do you pay any attention to him for? He never had any fun himself, and he doesn't want anybody else to have any."

The ducks were shaking their heads warningly and pointing their bills at the burdock plant. But Jinx pretended not to notice . "That old Wesley," he said. "If he was my uncle, you know what I'd do—I'd sew his bill up some night when he was asleep. Sew it with good stout thread and—"

At this point Uncle Wesley pushed aside the burdock leaves and waddled pompously out. "Ha, there you are, Wes, old mud-scoop," said Jinx. "I thought I could get you out."

The duck ignored him. "Alice!" he said. "Emma! Go into the house at once. I do not care to have you associating with these persons. I must say, I am grievously disappointed in you, grievously. I am astonished that you would sit quietly by and hear such insults heaped upon the head of your uncle. If *I* had heard anyone speak so of *my* uncle when *I* was a duckling—"

"You'd have torn him in pieces and used his backbone as a walking stick," Jinx interrupted. "Instead, you're going to quack him to death. Well—"

"Please, Jinx," Alice put in. "Don't tease Uncle Wesley any more." A year or so ago she and her sister would have rushed indignantly to their uncle's defence. But they no longer believed him to be the bold and fearless character he had always told them he was. They had looked up to him, admired him, taken his advice in everything—until one day they had seen him back down when he had tried to cheat a squirrel by selling him wormy nuts. After that, although they still believed that he was probably the wisest duck that ever lived, they no longer allowed him to tell them what to do every minute of the day.

"O.K.," said Jinx. "I take it all back, Wes. As a matter of fact, I've always considered you one of the most brilliant—no, no, I will say *the* most brilliant mind I have ever known. Why,

I was saying to Freddy only the other day—that Uncle Wesley, I was saying—why, he is so smart, I bet he could count right up to ten without stopping."

Uncle Wesley could swallow any amount of flattery, and at the beginning of Jinx's speech he had puffed out his chest and looked as important as possible. But at the end, he did have enough sense to see that the cat was making fun of him again, and he turned his back on him with an angry quack.

Jinx was going on, but Freddy said: "Oh, lay off, Jinx, will you? Look, Wesley, we came up to talk to you about something—"

"One moment," Uncle Wesley interrupted pompously. "Alice! Emma! What is all this about your being at the movies with some strange duck?"

"They weren't at the movies," said Freddy. "Jinx was kidding you."

Uncle Wesley pushed out his chest. "You will kindly not interfere in my domestic affairs, Freddy," he said. "I do not need an interpreter in getting an explanation from my own nieces."

"Very good, Wes," said Jinx. "Very well put. But you shut your bill and let Freddy talk, or

I'll knock it so crooked you'll have to be fed with a spoon."

"All we came up to say," said Freddy, "was that we're not too sure of that cat, Arthur, and we want to warn you to go slow with him. I know he's very pleasant spoken and entertaining, but—"

"That's enough," Uncle Wesley cut in coldly. "That's quite enough. You are speaking of one who has shown us a great deal of kindness. We are proud to call him our friend."

"Freddy is our friend too, Uncle," said Emma. "Hadn't we better listen to what he has to say?"

"You and your sister have led a very sheltered life, my dear," said Wesley. "You have wisely accepted my guidance in worldly affairs. I think that possibly I am as good a judge as Freddy of how you should choose your friends."

"Oh come on, Freddy," said Bill. "This guy will be no loss if Arthur does eat him. Friendship—hah! You know how such friendships end, don't you, Wes? Scrunch-scrunch, and a few feathers floating in the air."

"I don't care about Wesley," said Freddy,

"but Alice and Emma shouldn't be put in danger just because he hasn't any sense."

"Don't worry about us, Freddy," Alice said. "You've warned us and we promise to be very careful. Uncle Wesley is so loyal to his friends! You mustn't blame him."

"Alice!" said Wesley sharply. "I'll thank you not to apologize for me. I am not aware of needing any help in defending my opinions."

Jinx came to the end of his patience. "Oh, *gosh!*" he said exasperatedly. And he jumped up and pounced upon the duck, flattening him to the earth. "You silly old lunkhead!" he said, holding him down with one paw. "I'm going to whack some sense into you." And he rapped Uncle Wesley sharply on the head with his free paw. "I suppose if a rattlesnake smiled and took off his hat to you, you'd invite him to dinner. Well, you're going to make me a little promise, Wes. I'm going to hold you down and cuff you until you promise to have nothing further to do with Arthur."

Uncle Wesley shut his eyes and pulled his head down as close to his body as he could. He wished he was a turtle, so he could pull it right inside himself. But as he wasn't, he did the next

"You silly old lunkhead!"

best thing—he gave in. "I promise! I promise!" he quacked frantically.

He lay there for a minute after Jinx let him go, panting dramatically, and then he got up slowly. Alice and Emma waddled over to help him, but he pushed them aside and limped off towards his house. At the door he turned. "I warn you that I shall not keep that promise," he called. "You obtained it by force, and such a promise is not binding." And he went into the house.

"Oh, I give up!" said Jinx. "Well, if he wants to get eaten, let him climb right up on the platter and sit down. You girls be careful, that's all."

"We will, Jinx," said Alice. "And I think we can persuade Uncle Wesley to be careful too. At least we can keep him from going on any more long walks with Arthur. And by the way, it was funny your mentioning rattlesnakes. Because just yesterday Arthur and Uncle Wesley *saw* a rattlesnake. Up in the woods."

"There aren't any rattlesnakes around here," said Bill.

"Maybe a milk snake," said Freddy. "They look like rattlers. There's several of them living in the upper pasture. Very nice fellows, too."

"I'm sure Uncle Wesley couldn't be mistaken," said Alice. "He's very observant."

"We'd better talk to Arthur," said Freddy. He got up and swung into the saddle. "Come on, Jinx. So long, ducks. Now be careful, won't you?"

They found Arthur taking a sun bath on the flagstone at the foot of the porch steps. He said yes, that it was undoubtedly a rattlesnake that he and Wesley had seen.

Freddy looked at him sharply. "I see," he said. "And so if one of the ducks was to disappear, you would say that the rattler had undoubtedly caught it. Is that it?"

"Why, I think—" Arthur began. And then he stopped. "Oho!" he said. "I see what you're getting at. You think that I made up the rattler. You think I am planning to eat those ducks myself, and then blame it on the snake."

"Well," Freddy said. "We don't know anything about you, Arthur. You claim you left Margarine's because you were too tenderhearted to catch mice and so they wouldn't feed you. But how is it, then, that our friend

John found a bowl of milk out by their back steps the other night?"

Arthur didn't say anything. He was plainly very much embarrassed. He looked at Freddy and then he looked at Jinx, and then he cleared his throat several times and said: "H'm. Ha. Yes."

"Yes what?" said Bill sharply.

"Yes, I'm going to tell you the truth," Arthur said. "You see, I . . . No, no; I can't tell it to all of you like this. I couldn't tell it to anybody but another cat; it's too mortifying. Will you step aside with me, Jinx?"

So Jinx did. They whispered together for a minute, and then Jinx gave a loud yell of laughter. Arthur walked quickly away to the barn, and Jinx returned to his friends, fizzing with more yells which he was trying to hold back. He held a paw over his mouth for a minute, and then he said: "They've been feeding him all right. The reason he quit was—Oh, golly, it's a scream!" And he began fizzing again.

"Oh, for goodness' sake," said Cy. "If this is a private joke we'll go and leave you alone with it."

"No, no," said Jinx. "You've got to hear it.

The reason he quit was the name Mrs. Margarine called him. *Sweetie Pie,* she called him. Can you beat it? *Sweetie Pie!* For that big brute. She tied ribbons on him too. Pink ones. He couldn't take it. He said even the horses giggled whenever he walked past the stable. Oh boy, wait till the rest of the animals hear this."

"They mustn't hear it," said Freddy firmly. "I don't think we'd even better tell the mice, although it would probably stop them worrying about being eaten up. But if he's been going around with that name tagged to him, he's had enough kidding, and you know what they'll do if they hear it. I'd better go talk to him. I want to know more about the snake. I won't let him know you told us about his being '*Sweetie Pie.*' I'll just say you're satisfied about him, and we accept your word. We don't want him going around feeling embarrassed every time he sees one of us."

"I suppose you're right," said the cat. "But I hate to pass up a good joke."

"No joke is good if it hurts somebody's feelings," said Cy.

"My sakes, listen to the deacon!" said Bill. But he agreed with him just the same.

Chapter 5

Nothing much happened during the next few days, but all the animals had the feeling that something was going to happen—something big and unpleasant, probably. It was like the feeling you get just before a thunderstorm. "Everything is just too quiet," Freddy said. "We're all looking over our shoulders half the time, and getting ready to duck."

"There's a perfectly good reason for that," said Mrs. Wiggins. "Only we don't like to face it. We're all wondering if there really is a rattle-snake up by the woods. But if there is one, we'd almost rather not know it. We're like sick people who are afraid to call the doctor because he'll tell 'em what's wrong. I'll wager you haven't taken any steps yet to find out if what Arthur saw was a rattler or not."

Freddy thought a minute. "You're right," he said. "I didn't want there to be a rattler up there, so I pretended there wasn't one. But that's no way to act. Goodness, I'll see to it right away."

For some years Freddy and Mrs. Wiggins had operated what was probably the only animal detective agency in the East. They had a number of rabbits, mice, birds, spiders and other small animals on their payroll, and they could swing into action on a case at a moment's notice. Freddy called in their head operative, Rabbit No. 23, and gave him his instructions. Within an hour, half a hundred birds and small animals had been alerted; within five hours, No. 23 was back with his report . He saluted and said:

"Operative No. 23 reporting: Regarding supposed appearance of rattlesnake in woods above duck pond. Mr. E. Nibble, squirrel, states that he has several times distinctly seen a rattlesnake gliding through the grass. He is quite certain."

"I know Nibble," said Freddy. "He's kind of an alarmist. I don't think we can pay much attention to him. Go on."

"Yes, sir," said 23. "Theodore, frog, states that he was hissed at and pursued for some distance by a rattlesnake. But on being questioned more closely, he admits that it might have been a milk snake, trying to be funny. He says most milk snakes are practical jokers. Rabbits No. 18, 6 and 37, state that they have seen a rattler a number of times. Confirming this report are the statements of Mr. Horace Winship, peewee, Mr. Jefferson P. Hopp, redwing blackbird, and a number of other reliable witnesses among the bird population. Elbert and Emmeline, two young children of Mrs. Tilbury, rabbit, living in the upper pasture, are said to be missing, and there is a general feeling that this rattler is responsible." No. 23 paused. Then he said, "If I may make a suggestion, sir, perhaps I should go see this Mrs. Tilbury."

"I think you should," said Freddy. "Though I know her; her children are always getting lost. She's scatter-brained, even for—" He had been going to say "even for a rabbit," but thought it wouldn't be very tactful. He coughed, and said: "She has eighteen children, and if she counts them and finds there are only sixteen, she has hysterics right away, without even bothering to look in the next room. She enjoys making a fuss. My guess is that Elbert and his sister have been right there all the time."

No. 23 said: "Yes, sir. Shall I continue my investigation?"

"Not after you've seen Mrs. Tilbury," said Freddy. "It looks as if there really was a rattlesnake, and in that case it's too dangerous. I'd better take over the job myself now." Freddy couldn't help putting on a bold and fearless expression when he said this; he didn't really want to show off in front of 23, but the admiration in the rabbit's eyes was too much for him. After all, if you see that someone thinks you are a hero, you at least have to try to look like one.

No. 23 hopped off, and Freddy saddled Cy and rode up past the duck pond along the brook into the woods where there was a shady pool in which Theodore, the frog, lived. Freddy had spent many happy hours beside this pool, writing poetry, dreaming, occasionally just snoring the afternoon away. But today, though he dismounted, he didn't sit down on the mossy bank where he had composed so many of those famous and widely read verses. He drew his pistol and walked to the edge of the water. "Hey, Theodore!" he called.

There was a rustle in the bushes behind him, and he swung around.

"Don't shoot; I'll c-come quietly," said a voice, and the frog crawled out. "What's the idea, cowboy; afraid I'll jump you when you aren't looking?"

"No," said Freddy. "But I guess I'm a little nervous. I came up to look for that rattler."

"Oh, him!" said the frog. "He's chased me a couple of tut-tut, I mean times. I thought he was one of those smart-aleck milk snakes, and finally I squared off and gave him a poke in the nose. You'd have died laughing, F-Freddy. He just coiled up and stared at me with his mouth open, and then he backed off into the bub, bub—I mean bushes."

"Very funny," said Freddy. "And if he'd swallowed you, I guess you're the one that would have died laughing."

"Shucks, I can jump faster than any old rattler can strike," Theodore said. "And that's all bub, bub—I mean boloney about snakes hypnotizing you so you can't move. Any old snake tries to hypnotize me, I'll hypnotize him right back."

Before Freddy could say anything, a little hissing voice came from somewhere in the bushes. "All right, frog—let's see you do it. Look at me!"

They all looked. Cy reared and snorted, and Freddy backed slowly away from the bush under which they now saw the rattlesnake, coiled and ready to strike. But Theodore just stared at the snake, and even moved a step or two towards him.

"Hey, hold it, Theodore!" Freddy said, and he cocked his pistol. "Beat it, snake, or I'll blow you apart."

But the rattler, without removing his eyes from the frog, said in his sharp whisper: "You wouldn't kid me, would you, pig? I know there are no bullets in that gun."

Freddy stopped quickly and scooped up a handful of gravel which he poured down the pistol barrel. "Maybe this won't kill you," he said, pointing the gun again, "but I bet it will sting some."

"Take it easy, take it easy!" the snake protested. "Point that thing the other way. I wasn't going to swallow your friend. I just wanted to prove to him he doesn't know what he's talking about. Matter of fact, we can't hypnotize anybody. They just get so scared they can't move." His forked tongue flickered out mockingly. "Go on, frog, hop it. I'll call another day when you're not busy." And he uncoiled and started to glide away.

"Just a minute," said Freddy. "Are you planning to stay in this neighborhood?"

The front part of the snake turned around, and he flickered his tongue at Freddy. "Suppose I am—you want to make something of it, pig?"

"I'll make a snake's funeral of it, if you want to stay around here," Freddy said.

"My, my; such big talk!" the rattler sneered. "Unhealthy talk, too. Keep your eyes open, pig, when you walk through the long grass, or when you climb a stone wall. I'll be waiting there for you." He lowered his head and slid off through the undergrowth.

"You ought to have plugged him, Freddy," said Cy. "Mostly rattlers aren't so bad; they don't bother you unless you bother them first.

"Beat it, snake, or I'll blow you apart."

And they always rattle a warning before they strike. But this is a bad hombre—he'll be laying for you."

"I don't think so," Freddy said. "He was just trying to scare me. But we've got to get rid of him. We've never had rattlers in this part of the country, and we don't want any. Guess I'll consult Old Whibley."

Theodore, who had taken a standing leap into the water when the snake had turned away, now crawled out on the bank again. "Yeah," he said, "b-but how you going to do it? Look, Freddy—that gug-gug—I mean guy, he's got me scared. Can I come down and stay at the farm? Just until you get rid of the snake?"

"Sure. Only there isn't any water for you to sit in; you won't be very comfortable," Freddy said.

Cy said: "There's the watering trough in Hank's stable."

"That's right," said Freddy. "Only you want to be careful—Hank shuts his eyes when he drinks—he might swallow you."

"You warn Hank to be careful," said Theodore. "He'll be d-darned uncomfortable if he swallows me." He leaped straight from the ground up on to the saddle in front of Freddy, and they rode on.

Old Whibley, the owl, lived up in the woods with his niece, Vera. Freddy usually went to him for advice when he got in a jam, and it was good advice, but it was never much fun getting it, for Whibley was pretty grumpy and sarcastic. Today they found him in a good mood, however. He came out of his hole in the big tree at the first tap Freddy gave on the trunk, and floated down to perch opposite Cy's head. "Well, well," he said. "If it isn't the Masked Bandit of Roast Pig Gulch! Or is that your own face, and not a mask? Ah yes, I see it is now. Well, well; so you've brought me some lunch," he went on, staring with his big eyes at Theodore. "Very thoughtful."

"Oh, golly," said the frog, as he scrambled quickly up into the pocket of Freddy's thunder and lightning shirt. "What a life! I get out of one mess right into another."

"Out of the rattlesnake into the owl—if you'll permit me to adapt an old proverb," said Whibley.

"How's that?" said Freddy. "How did you know we'd seen a rattler?"

"Been watching that fellow for a couple of days," Whibley said. "Don't dare tackle him in the daytime, but I'll catch him in the open some night and then I'll have me a rattlesnake pie. Not as tasty as frog—" Theodore, who had poked his head out of the pocket, ducked hastily down —"but more filling."

"I hope you catch him soon," Freddy said. "What's he doing here anyway?"

"Forest fires up north this fall," said the owl. "Driven everybody out of that section of woods. Most of 'em gone back home now, but this fellow finds it easy to pick up a living around here —plenty of young rabbits and field mice—and he's in no hurry to leave."

"That's what I came to ask about," said Freddy. "We think he's after Alice and Emma. We thought you'd know how to get rid of him."

"Only one way," said Whibley. "Bite his head off. You want to try it?"

Freddy said: "I thought maybe you'd help me. But if that's all the advice you can give me—"

"I've got no advice to give you," said the owl, "except to keep away from him. Some night I'll get him. Until then, you and your friends keep out of his way."

Freddy knew that it was good advice. Just the same, he thought, there must be *some* way, if I could only think of it. I've got to do some thinking.

The only trouble with thinking was that he couldn't think really hard for more than a few minutes without dropping off to sleep. This is not peculiar to pigs; many people have the same trouble. Indeed some of them don't even know it, and they will rouse up and say: "My, I've been thinking hard; I'd better rest a while," when they've been snoring away like anything for the past hour.

Freddy had found that the best way to keep awake when he wanted to think was to go for a ride. Then if he dozed he fell off, and that usually woke him up again. Also, he could test any thoughts he got by trying them out on Cy, who had a good level head. Cy said that if some cowboys would talk things over with their horses, they would keep out of a lot of trouble. So they went for a ride.

And Freddy did get an idea. It came to him

just as he was trotting down the back road between the Big Woods and the Bean Woods. He dismounted and he and Cy and Theodore sat down by the roadside and talked it over; and then they went back home. They were just going across the barnyard when they heard a loud yell of laughter.

"Golly," said Freddy. "I know that voice!" And Cy said: "Yeah. Wonder who he's a making fun of today!" They rode around the other side of the stable and saw Billy Margarine doubled up with laughter on his tall scornful thoroughbred, and facing him, their heads lowered threateningly, were Mrs. Wiggins and her two sisters, Mrs. Wurzburger and Mrs. Wogus.

"Oh, gosh!" Billy gasped. "Oh, gee whiz! I never saw such funny looking animals!"

Freddy was good and mad. "Shut up!" he said, and he reined Cy up alongside the thoroughbred and pulled out his water pistol and squirted the entire contents into Billy's face. The boy was just opening his mouth to give another good yell of laughter, but the stream of water pushed the laugh down back his throat, and he began to cough and choke.

The thoroughbred neighed angrily and tried

to kick Cy, but the pony sidestepped nimbly, and then the cows closed in, threatening the horse with their horns. "You didn't need to bother, Freddy," said Mrs. Wiggins. "We can get rid of him. And we don't mind his laughing. It's kind of a compliment to be laughed at by anybody as foolish as he is."

"Oh, is that so!" said Billy, who had got his breath back. "Well, I'll show you how foolish I am!" And he raised his whip to slash at the cows. Then he dropped his arm. For a voice said: "What's going on here?" and Mr. Bean came around the corner of the barn.

The cows fell back respectfully. Jinx and Bill, with Charles, the rooster, and his wife, Henrietta, attracted by the rumpus, came up, and Mr. and Mrs. Pomeroy, the robins, flew down and started to perch on Freddy's shoulder, just as Theodore stuck his head out of the pig's shirt pocket. They darted off with a startled squawk.

"It's our cat," said Billy accusingly. "You've got him down here and he belongs to us."

"Cat?" said Mr. Bean. "Big tortoise-shell? I've seen the critter around. Yours, is he? Why don't you keep him at home?"

"I was riding by and I saw him and I came in to get him," said the boy. "But these animals wouldn't let me look for him."

"Probably didn't like your manners," said Mr. Bean. "I don't much myself. Why don't you call your cat? What's his name?"

"My mother says his name is—"

"Me-row-row-ro-ro-*o-o-ow*!" Jinx howled suddenly at the top of his lungs.

Everybody jumped. Except Mr. Bean. It took a good deal to make Mr. Bean jump—not that any of the animals ever tried, for he didn't like practical jokes. Now he turned and stared severely at the cat, then repeated his question.

"My mother calls him . . ." Billy began.

"Ma-a-a-a-a-*a-a-a*" went the goat.

Mr. Bean frowned. "What's the *matter* with you animals?" he demanded. "Haven't you been told times enough not to interrupt?" He stared at them all in turn, and they shifted uneasily. Bill and Jinx had interrupted because they didn't want the others to find out that Mrs. Margarine called Arthur "Sweetie Pie!" But the other animals were puzzled. They couldn't imagine what was going on. Fortunately Mr. Bean was a very smart man. He was proud of his animals because they could talk, but he was even prouder of them because they were almost always polite. And he knew that they would never interrupt like that unless there was a good reason. So he didn't ask again. He just said: "Never mind. You go on home. We don't want your cat. He'll come home when he gets ready."

"And I'll go home when I'm good and ready, too!" said Billy. "You can't order me around!"

"Well, all right," said Mr. Bean mildly. "You can stay right here until you take root, if you want to. Though maybe you'd better step back a little, so Mrs. Bean won't have to look at you every day from the kitchen window."

Billy turned red, and he said furiously: "I guess I'm no funnier to look at than this boy of yours." And he pointed to Freddy. Evidently he hadn't realized that Freddy, in his cowboy outfit, was a pig.

Mr. Bean took the pipe out of his mouth and a sort of fizzing creaking sound came out through his whiskers. The animals knew he was laughing. "My boy, hey?" he said. "Kind of takes after his pa, don't he? The same noble brow, the same classic features." He put the pipe back in his mouth and puffed so hard that it looked as if his whiskers were on fire. And the animals began to laugh. Henrietta started it with a hysterical cackle, and then Charles and Jinx and Bill chimed in, and in a few minutes the whole crowd was roaring. Mr. Pomeroy the robin, who wore glasses, was perched in the elm tree. He laughed so hard that he cried, and in trying to wipe his eyes with a claw he knocked his glasses off. They were not found for two days. Mrs. Wiggins bellowed until she was so weak that she had to be helped back to the cow barn by her sisters. And Cy shook so that Freddy could hardly stay in the saddle. And Mrs. Bean, coming out to see what all the racket was about, laughed until she had to sit down in the grass, although she had no idea what the joke was.

Billy had no idea what the joke was either. But he was no fool, and he realized that whatever it was, it was on him. He had never been laughed at like that before, and he didn't like it. He tried to make two or three smart remarks, but nobody heard them. And at last he couldn't stand it any longer, and he reined his horse around and rode out of the barnyard.

Mr. Bean went over and held out his hand

and pulled Mrs. Bean to her feet. He was still fizzing slightly.

" 'Tisn't really right to laugh at a boy like that, Mr. B.," she said.

"Taint really right to *have* a boy like that, if you come right down to it, Mrs. B.," he replied. "And so I'd say to Magarine himself if he was here. But now *our* boy—now there's a boy we can be proud of." And he began to creak and fizz all over again, until he choked on his pipe smoke, and Mrs. Bean had to pound him on the back. Which of course is the thing to do, because while it never helps anybody that is choking, it shows that you'd like to help if you knew how.

"And now, I'd take it kindly, Mr. B.," she said. "If you'd tell me just what it is I'm laughing at."

"Young Margarine," he said. "He thinks Freddy's our boy."

"Oh, my gracious," she said, and all at once looked very serious.

"What ails you?" said Mr. Bean. "You laugh before you know what the joke is, and when I tell it to you, you stop."

"Of course," said Mrs. Bean, "because Freddy will think we're laughing at him!" And she went right in and made a chocolate cake and took it up to the pig pen herself, so that Freddy wouldn't feel bad.

But of course he didn't feel bad. He had laughed as hard as anybody. But he was glad to get the chocolate cake just the same.

Chapter 6

The next morning Freddy went into the First Animal Bank, of which he was President, and drew out four dollars. He rode down to Centerboro and spent it all for gum, and then he came home and put up a sign on the cow barn, "Free Gum. Chew all day. Nothing to pay."

Even animals that can afford it seldom chew gum. Most of the Bean animals had tried it at one time or another, but said they couldn't see much in it. But of course when it was offered free, they saw no reason why they shouldn't take a stick or two. As a matter of fact, some of them were rather greedy, and took more than they could handle. Rabbit No. 74 got such a mouthful that he couldn't chew any more, and they had to hold him down and pry his jaws apart with a spoon to get the gum out.

Freddy didn't care how much they took. All he asked was that when they had chewed all the flavor out of the gum, they would give it back. Then they could have some more. So when the four dollars' worth was all chewed up, he and Jinx took it up in the loft over the stable and went to work. They shaped it into the form of a duck, and then rolled it around in a lot of feathers out of an old pillow and painted the bill and feet yellow. It looked quite a lot like a real duck. "Uncle Wesley to the life!" said Jinx. "Only it's got more brains."

"Doesn't it seem awful quiet around here?" Freddy said, when they brought their chewing gum duck downstairs. "Don't you notice it?"

"Sure," said Jinx. "It's all those jaws that have been chumping and chawing away for the past two hours. Now they've stopped. Hey, here comes Arthur!" He quickly covered the duck with an old sack as the big tortoise-shell strolled up.

"I'm obliged to you, Jinx," Arthur said. "And to Bill. I just couldn't take it if that awful name got out for all these animals to giggle over."

"It won't get out from us," said Jinx. "Not as long as you let the mice and birds alone."

"My dear Jinx!" Arthur protested. "It pains me deeply that you still distrust me. Ah, well, I shall hope to convince you in time." And he went on.

"Too blamed sanctimonious," Jinx said. "Well, I'll guard this duck and you go cut us out a couple of hosses."

Freddy had sent out several wasps as advance scouts to locate their enemy. Now as they rode up towards the duck pond Jacob came buzzing along and lit on the pig's nose. "Got him, Freddy," he said. "Cousin Izzy is keeping an eye on him. He's asleep on the top of the wall—right where that beech overhangs it—see?"

"Swell," Freddy said. "Couldn't be better for us. Cy, you and Bill go up along this side of the wall, and when you're opposite the beech, get into a quarrel and yell at each other. That will cover any sounds we make creeping up along the other side of the wall."

So Freddy and Jinx dismounted and circled around and crossed the wall into the woods some distance up. Then they crept cautiously down towards where Jacob had said the snake was sleeping.

Freddy could move pretty silently when he had to; Jinx of course made no noise at all. As they came closer they could hear their two friends on the other side of the wall.

"Yeah?" said Cy. "Well, all I can say is that anybody that could chew up and swallow an old pair of galoshes, buckles and all, hasn't got any very refined taste in food."

"Oh, is that so!" Bill retorted. "Well, let me tell you that there's more flavor in a good, well-aged galosh or boot than in a ton of that flat, prickly hay you smack your lips over."

The two friends had brought a bamboo fish-pole with them. To the end of it they had fastened their chewing-gum duck. When they were six or eight feet from the part of the wall where the rattler was asleep, they crouched behind some bushes and slowly pushed the duck towards the wall. As they did so, Jinx, with as much of a quack in his voice as he could manage, said, "Oh, come on, Emma. There isn't any snake around here."

Freddy who was behind Jinx, said: "Oh, do be careful, sister! He'll hypnotize you. Oh, oh! How can I ever face Uncle Wesley if I let my dear sister get swallowed." His voice didn't sound much like Emma's.

Jinx's whiskers twitched with amusement. He said: "Pooh, just let him try—that's all; just let him try!"

Then they saw the rattler. He raised his head from his coils and looked at the duck.

Jinx pushed it nearer. "Ha, ha!" he said. "I betcha he beats it the minute he sees me. Ah, there you are, old slither and snoop! Come on, do your stuff!"

Freddy crawled up carefully beside Jinx and whispered in his ear. "Alice doesn't talk like that, you dope. Quit using slang or he'll get on to you. She wouldn't say 'Betcha,' and 'do your stuff'!"

Jinx grinned. "Sorry," he murmured. "Guess I wasn't very ladylike. How's this?" And then he gave a silly giggle, and said: "Oh, sister, I

do believe the horrid creature winked at me!
Why, Mr. Snake! Tee-hee! I bet you're a terrible tease!''

"Oh, my goodness!" said Freddy under his
breath.

But the snake didn't seem to suspect anything. He perhaps had not had much experience with ducks, and may, like many other
people, have thought them much sillier than
they are. He raised his head higher and his
forked tongue flickered out angrily. Then he
just swayed there, staring at the duck.

Jinx managed to give a couple of little frightened quacks as he pushed the pole forward.
"You better not touch me!" he quavered. "If
you bother me, my Uncle Wesley will tear your
scales off!"

The snake gave a mean little snicker. "We
don't want to bother your uncle, so we won't
tell him, will we? Not now. Maybe I'll tell him
later when I get hungry again." And as Jinx
pushed the pole closer, the snake opened his
jaws and lunged at the duck.

A snake's jaws can stretch pretty wide. Half
of the duck disappeared into the rattler's mouth.
But as he closed his jaws and tried to swallow

the rest of it, his long fangs stuck fast in the gum.

For a second or two he didn't move, then he lifted his head and shook the duck hard. A few feathers flew off, and the gum just stuck tighter than ever. And then he flew into a rage, and he whipped and twisted and wriggled and thrashed about until he was exhausted. "O K," said Freddy, and he and Jinx came out and tied the rattler to their fishpole. They wound wire around him in a spiral and fastened it tight at the ends, and then they crossed the wall and got into their saddles and started home.

When they got there, they untied the snake and dumped him into a wooden box, covered with a piece of heavy window glass that Freddy had found in the loft. Before they put the cover on, Jinx held him down, and Freddy worked most of the gum out with a stick. "Tomorrow," he said, "we'll take him down to Centerboro and see if we can sell him."

"Who'd buy a rattlesnake?" Jinx said.

"Fred Whimper had two coons at his garage," Freddy said. "He said a lot of folks bought gas there just so they could look at the coons. I was thinking of Dixon's Diner. Folks that came in to look at him would have to at least buy a cup of coffee."

So next morning they hitched up Hank to the phaeton and loaded the box in and went down to Centerboro. But Mr. Dixon wasn't enthusiastic, even after Freddy offered to charge him only for the box, and throw the snake in free. "Folks don't want to look at snakes when they're eating," he said. "Makes their stomachs feel funny." Freddy tried a couple more places, and then drove home again.

He had to keep the snake in his study—which was the room in the pig pen where he had his typewriter and his easy chair and his books and papers. For Hank wouldn't have him in the stable, and Mrs. Wiggins said she and her sisters wouldn't get a wink of sleep if she knew he was in the cow barn. Freddy didn't mind, for the snake had had an interesting life, and he seemed eager to please—probably in the hope of being let go. He told Freddy in his harsh whispering voice tales of his exploits—some of them pretty hair-raising, for he was really a tough customer. Freddy enjoyed having him as a guest.

So Theodore didn't have to go live in Hank's watering trough after all. Before he started back

"O.K. rattler," said Freddy.

to his pool in the woods, he came up to the pig pen. He hopped up onto the snake's box, and put his nose down on the glass cover and stared so long and so hard with his bulging eyes that the snake got mad. "Go on away, will you?" he said. "It makes me nervous to be stared at."

"Oh, yeah?" said the frog. "And how abub—bout me? I suppose you weren't trying to make me nervous up in the woods?" And he kept right on.

The snake got more and more nervous; he tried striking at the glass, and he tried calling Theodore names, and he tried appealing to the frog's better nature—none of them had the slightest effect; there were those bulging eyes staring down at him without any expression at all in them. I guess you'd have been nervous yourself.

Finally the rattler got so jumpy and jittery that Freddy made Theodore stop. So the frog went home. But on the way he told everybody he met that he had hypnotized a rattlesnake. He made such a good story of it that for a week or so there was a crowd of small animals at the pool every day, wanting to hear about it, and hanging open-mouthed on his words.

Freddy wrote, offering the snake to his friend, Mr. Boomschmidt, who ran a circus. The circus was now in winter quarters in North Carolina. Mr. Boomschmidt replied that he'd be very happy to have a rattlesnake who would be company for Willy, the boa constrictor—at present the only snake in the show.

"And of course," Mr. Boomschmidt wrote, "any friend of yours, Freddy, is always welcome. But I think we'd better wait till the show comes north, for you can't ship him—the express company doesn't take rattlesnakes."

A good many animals dropped in at the pig pen to have a look at the rattler. Jinx wanted to charge them a nickel apiece just to look, and ten cents to bang on the box until he got mad and struck up at the glass. But Freddy said no, there was to be no teasing him. "It's never fair to pick on somebody that's helpless and can't fight back," he said. "Anyway, it's interesting to meet the animals that call. Those two sheep yesterday—do you realize they'd come all the way from Seneca Falls?"

John came in nearly every day to report progress in stirring up the farmers against the hunters. He had tried the same trick at the

Macy's—getting the hounds to chase him through a window; at Schermerhorns he had run through the milk house and managed to tip over two cans of milk; and at several other farms he had led the hunt across lawns and flowerbeds. "But it doesn't work, Freddy," he said. "Old Margarine pulls out his pocketbook and hands 'em enough to pay for the damage ten times over. And what happens? They tell him he's free to hunt over their land any time he wants to. We'll never put a stop to the hunting that way. I hate to bother Mr. Bean, but— what do you think, Freddy?—should I get 'em to chase me through here some morning? You could manage to have a window open, couldn't you? Get those four hounds in the parlor, and they'd stir it up, but good! I bet Margarine wouldn't get anywhere trying to pay Mr. Bean money."

"Mr. Bean wouldn't take his money," Freddy said. "He'd throw him off the place. But we mustn't bring Mr. Bean into it. Anyway, John, you get such a kick out of getting these people to chase you, why do you want to get rid of 'em?"

"I get a kick out of it—sure," said the fox. "Mainly, I guess, I want to get rid of 'em because instead of settling down nice and quiet, they want to run everything. It's like somebody joins a club, and he's a new member and ought to do things the way the rest of the club wants to. But instead, he starts right in telling them how *he* wants everything done and trying to boss them around."

"That's about it," Freddy said. "And he gives 'em each fifty dollars, and they say: 'Yes, sir; yes, sir,' and do just as he says. You can't blame 'em. Macy and Schermerhorn and the rest of them—they don't want these hunters galloping all over their fields, but it doesn't do much harm this time of year. And they need the money. Well, we'll have to try something different."

Chapter 7

One evening about a week later, Freddy was
sitting in a chair tipped back against the front
wall of the pig pen. He had on his cowboy outfit, which he wore nearly all the time now, and
he was strumming his guitar and singing in his
pleasant tenor a little song of his own composition about life on the wide prair-ee. Of course
Freddy had never seen a prairie, but he didn't

see why he shouldn't sing about it. "Most cowboy songs," he said, "are written by folks that
have never been west of Niagara Falls."

Georgie, the little brown dog, was curled up
in a deck chair beside him. Georgie was fond of
music, and often came up and asked Freddy to
sing for him. Sometimes he tried to join in, but
he didn't have a very good ear—Freddy found
it hard to keep on the key himself when Georgie
opened up.

"Sing the one that has the yodeling in it, the
serenade," said Georgie. So Freddy sang.

> *When the sun is gone,*
> *(Ooly ooly hey!)*
> *When the shadows fall,*
> *When across the lawn*
> *(Ooly ooly hey!)*
> *Bugs begin to crawl,*
>
> *By your window, sweet,*
> *(La di doodle day!)*
> *Then I strike my lute.*
> *I look pretty neat*
> *(La di doodle day!)*
> *Wearing my best suit.*

So I tell my love
      (Ho di wowly wow!)
Underneath the moon,
Cooing like a dove,
      (Ho di wowly wow!)
Slightly out of tune.

O, be mine! Be mine!
      (Bungle o li bang!)
Tell me I'm desired;
Give me but a sign;
      (Bungle o li bang!)
I am very tired.

It is very late.
      (Hi de heedle ho!)
Show me that you care
Do not make me wait:
      (Hi de heedle ho!)
Throw me out a chair.

Ah, she sleeps, alas!
      (Ooly ooly hey!)
Does not hear my song.
Dew is on the grass;
      (Ooly ooly hey!)
Better get along.

Silent is the lute;
    (Ho di wowly wow!)
Vain my tuneful pleas.
She doesn't give a hoot.
    (Ho di wowly wow!)
I am going to sneeze.

Freddy stopped suddenly. Up the slope from the barnyard came a procession of small animals. It was getting dark, and he couldn't see them very clearly, but they seemed to have perfectly round heads, and as they came closer, walking on their hind legs, he could make out that they were brandishing little knives in their paws.

Georgie gave a yelp and bolted into the pig pen with his tail between his legs. But Freddy laughed. "Come back," he called. "It's only the Horrible Ten. You've seen them before."

Georgie came to the door. "Yeah," he said. "But they always scare me. I'll stay right here."

The Horrible Ten was an organization of rabbits which Freddy had started in order to play a joke on Jinx. But rabbits don't often get a chance to scare people, and they had had so much fun that they had kept it up. They tied their ears down so that they wouldn't be recognized, and their knives were pieces of tin that Freddy had cut for them. But if they caught you outdoors after dark and went into their war dance, stamping around you in a circle and waving their knives and shouting their bloodthirsty chant—well, it was a pretty scary business.

When they got up to the pig pen the rabbits all sat down in a semicircle around Freddy's chair, and the Head Horrible—who was Freddy's detective assistant, No. 23—stepped forward and addressed them.

"Brother Horribles," he said, "gaze upon Mr. Frederick Bean."

The rabbits gazed at Freddy.

"Brother Horribles," said No. 23, "is it still your wish, as expressed by unanimous vote in the secret meeting of our order, to induct Mr. Frederick Bean into the order, with the title of Exalted Honorary Vice-Horrible, and all the privileges and emoluments thereto appertaining?"

"It is, Your Dreadfulness," said the rabbits.

So No. 23 hopped to Freddy's knee and reached up with his tin knife and tapped him on the shoulder. "Rise, Exalted Honorary Vice-Horrible!" he said solemnly.

"If I rise," Freddy thought, "23 will fall on his face." "But he didn't say it. He got up slowly, so that 23 could jump down.

"Brother Horribles," he said, "I am deeply appreciative of the great honor which you have bestowed upon me. I will endeavor to abide by the rules of the order, and to be, when necessary, as horrible as possible. In a purely honorary capacity, of course. For I understand that an *honorary* office is—well, just an honor. There is nothing that I have to do."

"Oh, nothing, of course," said No. 23 quickly. "Although," he went on after a slight pause, "we did hope that you might give us a little help in one matter."

"H'm," said Freddy thoughtfully, "as a strictly honorary Vice Horrible, I doubt it if I would be allowed to—"

"Oh, quit it, will you, Freddy?" said 23. "We thought you'd be pleased at being asked to join."

"So pleased that I'd agree to do a little work for you, hey?" Freddy said. "Oh, well, skip it. What is it you want?"

"Oh, I guess we went about this wrong, Freddy," said 23. "We thought maybe making you an honorary officer, we'd kind of soften you up so you'd be willing to help us. But we really did want you to be one of us. Because we're a lot bigger now, and we aren't just out for fun— we've got a real job to do." And he went on to say that all the rabbits in the countryside were disturbed about the foxhunters. The horses, galloping across fields, had smashed in a number of homes, and the hounds had dug up many more and they chased rabbits wherever they saw them. One of 23's cousins had been chased away up beyond Tushville, and had been three days getting home again, and was still confined to his bed, speechless from shock. "I doubt if he'll ever be the same rabbit again," said 23 mournfully.

"But foxhounds chase foxes, not rabbits," Freddy said.

"Oh, yeah?" said 23. "That's what they tell you. But when those Margarines aren't around they'll chase rabbits or cats or woodchucks or— why, I've seen 'em even trying to dig a chipmunk out of a stone wall. Fine business for a full-grown hound!"

"Let me see."

"Well, what do you want me to do?" Freddy asked.

"We're the Horrible Twenty now instead of the Horrible Ten," said the rabbit. "So we need a new chant to go with our war dance. The old one—

> *We are the Horrible Ten,*
> *Neither animals nor men—*

that doesn't go any more. It has to be: We are the Horrible Twenty."

"H'm," asid Freddy. "Not near as good. But let me see. Twenty, plenty—guess there's only one rhyme.

We are the Horrible Twenty,
Of ferocity, boy! we've got plenty!
Plenty, sufficient and lots!

H'm; lots, knots, plots—" He went on slowly.

"We weave diabolical plots
To capture our victims alive.
And when we have caught four or five
We sing and we yell and we dance and we haul
Them down to the kitchen and chop them up
    small,

Add lemon and pepper and salt, and a dash
Of Worcestershire sauce. For enemy hash
Is the dish of all dishes that crowns all our
    wishes,
We eat it for breakfast and dinner and lunch,
We munch and we crunch, we gobble and
    scrunch,
We—"

"Hey, wait a minute," said 23. "This isn't any war song; it's a description of you eating dinner."

"Oh, come, come!" said Freddy. "Is that polite?" Then he sighed. "I wish though I didn't think about food so much. Gracious! and now I'm smacking my lips over eating up my enemies! That's pretty bad." He sighed again. Talking about eating, even such an unappetizing dish, had made him hungry. "Look boys," he said, "you go along. I'll work out something for you. Come up tomorrow and I'll have it ready."

So the Horrible Twenty trudged off down the hill, and Freddy went in and he and Georgie had some cookies and milk.

Over this snack—if you can call it a snack when you eat three dozen cookies at a sitting—

they chatted about local affairs, but as both of them had their mouths full most of the time, neither understood much of what the other said. They were licking up the last crumbs when Mr. J. J. Pomeroy, the robin, flew in. He and his wife and children usually dropped in every few days and did a little cleaning for Freddy—that is, they ate up the crumbs, which owing to his habit of working at his typewriter with a cookie or a sandwich in one hand, were pretty well strewn all over everything.

But Mr. Pomeroy hadn't yet found his glasses, and couldn't tell a crumb from a carpet tack. He had come to warn Freddy that Mr. Margarine and Billy had just ridden into the yard.

Freddy jumped up, and a shower of crumbs flew off his lap. "Thanks, J. J. Come on, Georgie. Let's go down."

In the barnyard Mr. Margarine, on his tall horse, was looking down at Mr. Bean, who stood beside him. Billy was walking his horse slowly around, inspecting the cowbarn and the henhouse, and not listening to what the men were saying.

"I'm sorry you take it that way, Bean," Margarine was saying. "From our terrace that red barn of yours sticks up like a sore thumb. Spoils the view entirely. Mrs. Margarine is quite sick about it. And I'm not asking you to tear it down. If you'd just consent to have it repainted a nice green—naturally I'll have the job done myself—"

"Sorry I can't do it," Mr. Bean interrupted. "Like to oblige you. But the barn's always been red. Red it'll stay."

"But what's the difference?" said Mr. Margarine, and his thin mouth drew down at the corners. "A green barn is—"

" 'Tain't a barn any more," put in Mr. Bean. "Red's a natural color for barns. Paint it green, it'd mix me all up. Like as not I'd think it was the chicken coop, think somebody'd stole the barn, waste a lot of time hunting for it."

It was dark in the barnyard; Freddy couldn't see Mr. Bean's face, but he would have bet there was a good strong twinkle in his eye.

"Well, if you want to be stubborn," Mr. Margarine said.

"I do," said Mr. Bean. "One of the few pleasures I can afford."

"I'm not so sure you can afford it," replied the other. His voice was threatening. "I've made you a perfectly fair proposition. If you don't choose to accept it you needn't be surprised if you have to take the consequences."

Mr. Bean nodded. "One of 'em bein' that the barn stays red. And now that that's settled—"

"You old fool!" Mr. Margarine snapped. "Don't you realize who I am? Don't you—"

"Stop right there!" Mr. Bean did not raise his voice, but it was suddenly as cold as ice. "We're kind of old-fashioned in these parts. You've come in here and tried to change a lot of things. We've put up with it—some of us because we want to be friendly and helpful, and others because you handed out money so free. We hoped we could get along with you. But I guess you can only get along with folks that stand up to attention and say 'sir.' We don't do that up here much—"

"No?" said Mr. Margarine with a sneer. "Your friends, Witherspoon and Macy and the rest of them seem willing enough to do as I want them to. And they're paid well for it. They're smart; they know which side their bread is buttered on."

"They're smarter than you think," said Mr. Bean. "Sure, they like your money. But they don't like being pushed around. And before long they're going to decide that no money is big enough to put up with it any longer—" He stopped, as a sudden great cackling and laughing broke out over by the henhouse.

While his father talked, Billy had been exploring the barnyard. The henhouse had what was rather an unusual feature, a revolving door. With twenty-seven children running in and out all day long, and often forgetting to close the door after them, it isn't surprising that it had been hard to keep the place warm; and when Henrietta had complained of the cold, Mr. Bean had had the door put in. It was this door that had caught Billy's eye. And as he watched the door whirl and the chickens run in and out, he began to laugh.

It was a perfectly natural thing for him to laugh at, but the animals had had about enough of Billy's laughter. And now they knew how to stop it. Charles, who was sitting on the henhouse roof, and Jinx and Bill, who were standing nearby, watching Mr. Margarine, started it. They began to laugh. Then the chickens rushed out and Freddy and Georgie and Robert, the collie, came up and they all joined in. They stood around Billy and laughed at him, and their laughter was three times as loud as his.

Billy couldn't take it. He turned and rode over to his father and, pointing his finger back at the henhouse, evidently accused the animals of making fun of him. But nobody could hear what he said, for the animals had followed him, and the cows and Cy and Hank had come out, and even Sniffy Wilson, the skunk, and his family, who had come down to call, joined the crowd, and they formed a circle about Billy and his father and just laughed.

The animals closed in slowly, keeping one eye on Mr. Bean, who was inside the circle too, of course. If he had shown even the faintest sign of disapproval, they would at once have stopped and gone away. But he didn't move a finger—just stood there in the deepening twilight looking up at Mr. Margarine.

The animals laughed for a full minute—and a minute is a long time when you're being laughed at. And if Billy couldn't take it, neither could Mr. Margarine. Probably nobody had ever dared to laugh at him before. He raised his whip threateningly as if to cut at Mr. Bean. "Drive these animals away!" he shouted.

Probably he didn't really intend to strike Mr. Bean. But the animals weren't taking any chances with him. The laughs turned into growls, and they moved in quickly. Hank and Cy and the cows shoved against the horses and the dogs nipped their heels and herded them towards the gate. The smaller animals crowded to get a bite or a scratch if they had a chance. Mr. Margarine and Billy tried to use their whips, but they were pushed around so violently that it was all they could do to stick to their saddles.

They were herded through the gate, and it was there that Charles performed probably the most spectacularly heroic act of his entire career. The rooster always talked very big, but when the time came to act he was usually somewhere else. Once in a while, though, when he was good and mad, he would become completely reckless. And now, as the Margarines turned out into the road, Charles took off from the henhouse roof, sailed across the barnyard, and flew straight into Mr. Margarine's face. Squawking angrily, he beat at the man with his wings, pecked him twice on the nose, and ended by knocking off his elegant derby hat, which fell into the dirt and was trampled by the horses.

And then to complete their defeat, as they started up the road towards home, Freddy pulled out his pistol and fired two of his blank cartridges in the air.

As the sound of galloping hoofs died away, the animals fell back. Mr. Bean was still standing in the middle of the barnyard. And then as they watched to see what he would do, he walked across and picked up the battered derby hat and set it carefully on the gatepost. He looked at it a moment critically, then they saw him bend over and slap first one knee and then the other, and they heard the sound of his creaking laughter.

Chapter 8

Mr. Margarine wasted no time. Late the next morning Sheriff Higgins came rattling out from Centerboro in his old car. As he shut off the engine and climbed out, Freddy came running down from the pig pen, for the sheriff was an old friend.

"Hi, sheriff," said the pig. "How's everything at the jail?"

But the sheriff just peered blankly at Freddy, then pulled out a paper and held it close to his nose, glancing every now and then at the pig as if comparing him with a written description.

After a minute he looked up. "Is your name Charles?" he asked, and as Freddy grinned and started to say something: "Charles," he said. "A rooster. With a sharp beak and blue and green tailfeathers." He looked Freddy over as if he had never seen him before. "You've got the beak all right. But no tailfeathers. Turn around —no, no tailfeathers at all."

Freddy thought it was some kind of a joke at first, but the sheriff's manner made him think that there was something serious back of it. He decided not to laugh, but to play up for a minute or two.

"No, sir," he said. "You wish to see this Charles?"

"I got a warrant for his arrest," said the sheriff. "Also for some queer kind of animal—half pig and half cowboy, according to this description here. Ever see any such critter around here?"

Freddy said no, he hadn't.

"I have to do my duty," the sheriff said. "If I was to see—*and* recognize—either of these animals, I'd have to take 'em down to the jail. Hold 'em for trial. Seems they attacked this here rich Mr. Margarine last night. Tried to scalp him, shot at him, pecked his nose and damaged his nervous system."

"I heard something about it," said Freddy cautiously. "But how could he prove that they attacked him?"

"Man's got as much money as he has can prove most anything," said the sheriff. "But I guess there ain't any trouble to prove it. Seems Mr. Bean saw it all, and he wouldn't lie about it, even to keep his animals out of jail."

"No, I suppose not," said Freddy. "What do you think will happen to them—if you catch them, that is?"

"Why, they'll be tried before Judge Willey, likely. Tried and convicted and sentenced to— oh, probably they'll get off with a couple years at hard labor. Peckin' a rich man's nose—that's a pretty serious crime in this state. And shootin' at a rich man—why for shootin' at a poor man I've seen 'em get six months. As for attemptin' scalpin'—well, we ain't had a scalpin' case as long as I've been sheriff. Hard to tell how a jury'll feel about it." He peered at the paper again. "Forgot my readin' glasses, I can't make out the descriptions of these criminals. Maybe you'd like to read 'em to me." He held the paper out.

Freddy said: "I'm afraid I haven't got time just now. There's something I have to do."

The sheriff nodded. "Good thing to do things quick if they have to be done. Folks that fiddle around and put things off, they sometimes end up in jail." He looked hard at Freddy and nodded again. "Like these criminals. If they're smart, they'll take to the woods for a while. They'll know that if I don't catch 'em today, I'm too busy a man to go chasing them. Well, good day to you. I'll go in and see if Mr. Bean knows where they are." And he started for the house.

Ten minutes later he was still inside the house, helping Mr. Bean with a large pot of coffee and a jar of doughnuts, and he didn't see Freddy mount Cy and ride across the barnyard and up towards the woods. The pig had on his cowboy outfit, his guitar was slung at his back, and on the saddle before him perched Charles.

The two fugitives from justice rode up through Mr. Bean's woods, across the back road and into the Big Woods. There was an old abandoned house, the Grimby house, in the Big Woods, where Freddy had hidden out once before. That night he slept on a pile of old burlap bags in the attic, while Charles perched in a tree outside, and Cy trotted back to the farm with messages for Freddy's friends which there hadn't been time to deliver before leaving home.

Cy spent the night at the farm, but was back at the Grimby house by sun-up, to report that the sheriff had gone back to Centerboro after assuring himself that neither Charles nor Freddy was anywhere on the place. Freddy was pleased at the news, for he felt sure that the sheriff wouldn't make much of an effort to arrest him; but a report brought by Mr. J. J. Pomeroy later in the morning was disturbing. The Pomeroys had flown down to Centerboro and hung around the jail on the chance of picking up some bits of news that would be of use to Freddy. They had been sitting on the windowsill of the sheriff's office when Mr. Margarine had come in. "Are you going to sit here twiddling your thumbs," he had demanded, "while these ruffians who attacked me are still at liberty?"

"That question falls into two parts," the sheriff had replied. "As to twiddling my thumbs, I don't know how to twiddle 'em, and that's the truth. So the answer to that is no. As to whether I'm going to sit here—yes, I am. I've got work to do and I'm going to sit here and do it."

Mr. Margarine got mad and accused him of not doing his duty, but he only answered mildly that there was a great deal more duty around the place than there was sheriff. "If you want all that duty attended to, you got to provide me with about a dozen deputies," he said.

"Very well," said Mr. Margarine. "Swear me in as deputy. I'll bring in those two myself."

"I guess the sheriff didn't want to do it much," said Mr. Pomeroy, "but he couldn't get out of it. He'd seen us there on the sill and knew who we were, I guess. For when old Margarine had gone he came over and looked out the window and sort of talked to himself. 'I'd like to warn that pig,' he said, 'bein' he's a friend of mine. But I'm the sheriff—I can't do it.' So we flew right out to tell you."

This was not the first time Freddy had had to go into hiding. Twice before not only the sheriff but the state troopers, had been after him; but on both those occasions he had been innocent. "This time," he said, "I'm guilty, because I really did fire off my pistol. And so are you, Charles. You really pecked his nose and knocked off his hat. If they catch us—Hey!" he said suddenly. "That hat! We can use it. J. J., tell Georgie if he can find it, to bring it up tonight after dark."

Later in the day Mr. Pomeroy returned to report that Georgie would bring the hat. But other information which he brought was more disquieting. Mr. Margarine had called on Mr. Bean's neighbors—the Macys, the Schermerhorns, the Witherspoons, the Halls—and had offered a large reward for Freddy's capture. All had agreed to help.

"You can't exactly blame them, Freddy," said Mr. Pomeroy. "I heard Mr. Schermerhorn talking about it. 'I don't like to go against Bean and his animals,' he said. 'But that Freddy's awful smart. He's got out of it before all right when they were after him, and he'll get out of it this time. So what's the harm in our getting a chunk of old Margarine's money? I don't specially like the man, but I do like the crackle of those fifty dollar bills.' "

"The trouble is, they're not mad at Margarine," Freddy said. "If we could get 'em really good and sore. . . . H'm, I wonder. Look, J. J.; tell Robert to come up with Georgie tonight. And Hank. And Jinx on that wild bucking broncho of his. We'll meet here at nine o'clock."

So that evening when they had all come, Freddy got up on the porch of the Grimby house and addressed them.

"I've asked you to come up because I need your help," he said, "but it is not just help for me—it's help for Mr. Bean, too. Because he's the only farmer in this neighborhood who won't knuckle down to Mr. Margarine. Margarine couldn't do much if all the farmers stood together against him. So one thing we can do is to get all the farmers mad at him. And this is how to do it."

Freddy told them his plan, and they agreed that it was a good one. But Hank said: "I dunno, Freddy: I'm pretty old to go careerin' around the country in the middle of the night. Step in a woodchuck hole, likely, and bust a leg."

Freddy started to speak, but Charles, always

Freddy got up . . . and addressed them.

ready on the slightest excuse to deliver an oration, fluttered up on the porch railing.

"My friends," he said. "You know, I know,
we all know that danger threatens our friend
and protector, William F. Bean. Does that name
mean nothing to you, gentlemen? Are we to
stand idly by while that rich and vicious scoundrel, Elihu P. Margarine, brings the ancient and
honorable house of Bean crashing down in ruin
about our heads? What is a leg, what are a dozen
legs, when the honor of Bean is at stake?"

"I ain't got a dozen," Hank put in. "I only
got four."

"Only four!" Charles exclaimed. "Only four!
I have only two, yet how willingly I would sacrifice both for our noble benefactor! Ah, yes,
would that I had a dozen, nay, a hundred legs
to risk in this desperate venture! My friends,
the clarion call to battle has sounded, the—"

"Oh, be quiet!" Henrietta had appeared at
the edge of the clearing. "I guess it's a good thing
I came up here," she said as she came forward.
"Charles, get down off that railing! And Freddy
—you see here: if there's going to be any fighting, I want it distinctly understood that Charles
is to have no part in it. You!" she exclaimed,

turning upon her husband. "A fine mess you've got yourself into, and the sheriff hunting for you like a common criminal! You know where you'll end up, don't you?—on a platter with a lot of dumplings, that's where!"

"Just a minute, Henrietta," said Freddy. "In the first place, Charles isn't going with us to-night. And in the second place, what we're doing, we're doing for Mr. Bean." And he told her the plan.

Since Charles was not in any danger, Henrietta had no further objections. Hank had as usual been greatly moved by Charles' stirring speech, and he said that he guessed he'd be willing to sacrifice a leg if it was for Mr. Bean. "Only I hope it's my left hind one," he said. "That one's so rheumatic it ain't much use anyway."

Charles and Henrietta stayed at the house, in case any messages came up from the farm, and the rest of the animals cut down to the back road, and along it until they could see the Schermerhorn farmhouse. There were no lights; the Schermerhorns had gone to bed; but Freddy said that it wasn't quite late enough, so they waited another hour. Then Freddy got up.

"O K," he said; "Let's go." And he swung himself into the saddle.

Jinx leaped on to the sacks that were tied to Bill's back, and Hank ranged alongside.

"All right, Robert," said Freddy. "You and Georgie know the course we're going to take. Don't get too far ahead. And don't bark; try to bay like hounds."

"I'm a collie," said Robert. "I can't sound like a hound."

"How about you, Georgie?" Freddy asked. "You claim to be part wolfhound; can't you bay?"

"We're quiet when we hunt," said Georgie. "Silent and sinister, that's the family motto. But I can howl, if that'll help."

"Both of you better howl some," said Freddy. "We want to make as much of a disturbance as possible. Go ahead, we're right with you. Yoicks!" he shouted. "Yippee!"

"Orooloooloooooo!" howled Georgie, and he and Robert dashed down the slope towards the Schermerhorn farm, with Bill and Cy and Hank thundering along behind them.

Chapter 9

If it hadn't been a dark night Freddy's scheme would have had small chance of success. Freddy, mounted on Cy, might at some distance have been taken for Billy Margarine, but no one could have seen any resemblance to Mr. and Mrs. Margarine in Jinx, riding goat-back, or the riderless Hank. Nor were Georgie and Robert, in their role of foxhounds, very convincing, either to the eye or the ear.

But as the yelling hunt poured through their

gate, the Schermerhorns, roused from their first sleep to run to the window, made out only a troop of dim figures which circled the house twice, trampling flower beds, cutting up the lawn, and kicking over whatever stood in their way, and then galloping off across the fields towards Witherspoons'.

"Good heavens," said Mrs. Schermerhorn, "I think we've had about enough of these Margarines. Don't they ever sleep? I miss my guess if that crash we heard wasn't that pink soup tureen Louella gave us for a wedding present. I left it out for you to transplant those geraniums into it. If you'd done as I asked you it wouldn't have got broken."

"Oh, Margarine'll be around in the morning to pay for the damage," said Mr. Schermerhorn. "I guess we can put up with losing a little sleep for what he'll pay."

"There isn't any money he could pay would make me put up with losing that tureen," said Mrs. Schermerhorn. "And if you hadn't shilly-shallied and put off. . . ." She went on for some time.

In the meantime the hunt swept on towards the Witherspoon farm. It is fun to gallop

through the night, yelling at the top of your
lungs, and even Hank had forgotten his rheu-
matism, and snorted and pranced like a colt.
Though where he had got the idea that such
cries as "Thar she blows!" or "Forward, the
light brigade!" were the sort of thing that foxhunters should shout, nobody could figure out.

Freddy, galloping alongside him, said, "I'm
glad you've entered into the spirit of the chase,
Hank."

"Pike's Peak or bust!" shouted Hank. "Yeah,
I guess I have. Only what are we chasing?—On
to Richmond!" he roared.

Twice around the Witherspoon house they
went, then down to Macy's where they drove
through the big barn with yells and a series of
crashes that brought the entire Macy family out
of their beds as if they had been touched off like
rockets. Then on to the Halls', where they tore
yelling three times around the house like In-
dians attacking a wagon train.

It was always hard to get Hank started, but
once you had him started it was just as hard to
stop him again. The Halls were the last call
Freddy had planned to make, but Hank would
have gone right on through Centerboro, wak-

ing up everybody from Mr. Muszkiski to the Reverend Dr. Wintersip. Freddy managed at last to calm him down, although as on the way home they passed Mrs. McMinickle's little house, Hank went up on the porch and banged on the front door with a big hoof. "Get up! Get up!" he shouted. "The British are coming!" Fortunately Mrs. McMinickle was not at home, but her little dog, Prinny, came to the window and barked furiously. "There's one who'll stand off the redcoats if they get funny with him," said Hank with a grin. But after that he quieted down and went on home, while Freddy rode back to the Grimby house.

Things moved slowly for the next few days, but they moved in Freddy's favor. The farmers supposed of course it was the Margarines with their hounds who had made such a racket, and they waited expectantly for Mr. Margarine to show up with a fist full of crisp bills. When after two days he didn't appear, they began to get mad. And when on the third night the hunt came roaring down and lifted them out of their beds again shortly after midnight, they called up Mr. Margarine and demanded to know what he was going to do about it.

Of course Mr. Margarine denied that he and his hounds had been out on either of the nights in question. But his hat had been found on the Macy porch—and after all, who else kept hounds and chased foxes on horseback all over their fields? They didn't believe him.

Mr. Margarine was no fool. He was pretty sure that Freddy was back of these disturbances. Where he was wrong was in thinking that Mr. Bean was back of Freddy. He went to see the Macys and the Witherspoons and the rest of them and said flatly that he was certain it was Mr. Bean who had led the midnight hunt, and who was trying to discredit him. But they just laughed. Mr. Bean wasn't that kind of man, they said. Freddy now—yes, it could very well be Freddy. And they laughed and said that Freddy had a great sense of fun. Mr. Margarine got madder and madder.

After that he and Billy rode out nearly every night, looking for Freddy, hoping to intercept the hunt. They left the hounds at home, and carried shotguns across their saddles. But Freddy was in no danger, for Old Whibley kept him informed which way they were riding. But though he rode a good deal at night, he didn't lead any more midnight hunts to the different farms, for the farmers had shotguns handy now, too, and would use them.

Late one afternoon the Horrible Twenty came up to the Grimby house. Freddy was sitting on the porch thinking. They squatted around him in a circle and began to chant over and over: "We are the Horrible Twenty. We are the Horrible Twenty. We are the Horrible Twenty."

Pretty soon Freddy opened his eyes. "All right, all right," he said irritably. "I know who you are."

"We are the Horrible Twenty. We are the—"

"Oh, shut up!" Freddy said. "Can't you think of anything else to say?"

Rabbit No. 23 stepped out in front of them and held up his paw, and when they had stopped, he said: "No, we can't. Because you promised to make up something for us, but you never did it."

"Ah," said Freddy, "I see. And you're going to keep on repeating that one line until I either go crazy or write you a new chant?"

"Yes!" said all the Horribles together.

"O K," he said. "But there are more than

twenty of you here now. Twenty-six, is it?—if you'd only stand still a minute."

"We are standing still," said 23. "And there are twenty-five of us now."

"Well, that won't do! We are the Horrible Twenty-five. Hardly a man is now alive . . . No, no; can't make anything of that. Let's make it thirty. There'll probably be thirty members soon. Let's see. We are the Horrible Thirty. Wild eyed, ferocious and dirty. That's not bad. Go play tag out there for a while, will you?— I can't write with fifty eyeballs rolling around at me."

So they went down the steps and played games, and after a little while Freddy came down to them. "How's this?" he asked and re-cited:

"We are the Horrible Thirty,
Wild-eyed, blood-thirsty and dirty!
Our manners are simply atrocious—
Impudent, rude and ferocious.
At home, disobedient creatures;
In school, we throw things at teachers.
Punished, we stick out our tongues,
Scream at the top of our lungs.

Folks we don't like, we attack 'em,
Out come our knives and we hack 'em.
Even the bravest are nervous
When in the gloom they observe us.
As through the trees we come creeping
Even the boldest start weeping.
Even the calmest will bellow,
Shake like a bowlful of jello.
Oh, how we laugh when they holler!
Sometimes they offer a dollar
Not to be hashed up and fried.
Often we've laughed till we've cried,
Keeping—of course—right on hashing,
Paying no heed to their thrashing.
All we want's enemy hash;
Don't give a hoot for their cash."

There was a lot more, but as it was even more bloodthirsty, it is not set down here.

The Horribles liked the chant, and they tramped around the clearing for some time practicing it. Then they decided that they would go down and try it out on Mr. Margarine, but Freddy put a stop to that. "Too dangerous," he said. "You wait; I know you'd like to help Mr.

"O gimme my boots and gimme my saddle."

Bean, and maybe later we can figure out some way. Stick around."

Freddy went back up on the porch and picked up his guitar. He sang *Believe Me If All Those Endearing Young Pigs,* and he sang *The Old Pigs at Home,* and then he struck a minor chord and swung into a very mournful cowboy song of his own composition.

O gimme my boots, and gimme my saddle,
For back to the range I'm goin' to skedaddle.
    Yip, yip, yippee! O my! O my!
O saddle up the pinto and saddle up the grey,
For I ain't goin' to stay here—no, I ain't goin'
        to stay
Where the skies are dreary and the folks ain't
        gay.
    O my!

        Yip, yip!

        O my!

I'm goin' back home now: I'm going back home,
Where I never use a toothbrush, never use a
        comb.
    Yip, yip, yippee! O my! O my!

*Goin' back to the prairie, for the only sound
     that'll*
Make me happy again is the rattlesnake's rattle
As he sidewinds along, a-chasin' of the cattle.
   O my!

   Yip, yip!

   O my!

The Horribles, who had come up to listen, were much affected and some of them broke right down and cried. Freddy realized that this was a great compliment to his singing, and so he put as much sadness into his voice as he could. He put so much in that he began to feel the tears coming to his own eyes, and a lump get into his throat, and then all at once a big sob cut the song short and he had to stop.

"I'm sorry," he said. "This song—it always makes me want to cry. I'm sure I don't know why it should. I don't know why I should get so sad longing to get back to somewhere I've never been. Funny how you can cry about wanting something that you don't want at all."

No. Eleven said: "It was your voice—it was so sorrowful it made us all cry."

"Yeah," said Freddy, "and then I saw you crying and that made me even sadder. My goodness, it's a good thing I stopped—we'd have all ended up crying ourselves into fits. I better sing something lively."

He took up the guitar again, but before he could begin, Bill, with Jinx on his back, came galloping into the clearing. The cat leaped from the saddle and bounded up the sagging porch steps. "Bad news, Freddy," he said. "Last night that Margarine rode over and told Mr. Bean that if any of us animals were found on his land, we'd be shot, and then he and the boys, they went up to the pig pen and searched it. Guess maybe they thought you were hiding there. Anyway they threw things around quite a lot. Mr. Bean couldn't stop 'em. Margarine had a deputy's badge or star or something."

"Oh, golly!" said Freddy. "I hope they didn't lose any of my papers. My poems—all my poems; I've been selecting the best ones to be published in a book. The Poetical Works of Frederick Bean, Esq. I must go down there right away."

"You can't, you dope," said Jinx. "Margarine's watching the place day and night. And he's advertised for a detective. Look here." And he handed Freddy an advertisement clipped from the Centerboro *Guardian*.

WANTED—*Man for light detective work. Able to ride horse. Good pay. Must provide own disguises.* Phone Margarine, Centerboro *884.*

"Well, he hasn't got his detective yet, if that was just in this morning's paper. Hey, Cy!" he shouted. And as the pony came up, he leaped into the saddle and in spite of the protests of Charles and Bill and Jinx and all twenty-five Horribles, he galloped off through the trees.

Chapter 10

Freddy knew that he was running into danger,
but the thought that his precious poems might
be strewn about and trampled into the dirt
made him reckless. He rode straight down to
the pig pen. He saw nobody, but for safety's
sake he had Cy come inside with him, although
when both of them had crowded into the little
room they couldn't look around much or see
anything but each other. Finally Freddy had Cy
go outside again.

As far as he could see, his papers hadn't been disturbed. He was looking them over when the four mice came out from under the desk. "Hi, Freddy," said Eek. "We came to kind of look after things for you. We thought we'd better when we heard the Margarines had been here. We sort of picked up after 'em. Your papers were all over the floor."

"Crumbs, too," said Eeny. "Peanut butter cookie crumbs. When did you sweep last? Mrs. Bean hasn't made any peanut butter cookies since last spring."

"We wouldn't have dared come up if the snake had been here," said Quik. "But when we heard—"

"The snake? What do you mean?" Freddy exclaimed. He dashed into the other room where he kept the disguises he used in his detective work. The box was there, but the glass was pushed aside and the rattlesnake was gone.

The mice had followed him in. "The Margarines let him out," said Quik. "They thought you were in the box I guess, and they shoved the glass off and poked a flashlight in to look. You ought to have heard 'em yell! Mrs. Wiggins came to the barn door and saw 'em galloping off as fast as they could lick."

"Where'd the rattler go?" Freddy asked. "That's the important thing."

"Nobody saw him go. But we had the Pomeroys scout ahead of us when we came up, and the wasps had been in here and said he wasn't inside, so we knew we were safe coming up."

Freddy thanked them warmly, and then went through his poems. One was missing. It was one of a series on "The Features" and it was about the eyes. Freddy couldn't find it anywhere.

He was looking for it under the bed when Cousin Augustus who had been posted as a sentinel at the window, gave a loud shout of warning. At least it was loud for a mouse. Freddy looked out and saw Mr. Margarine and Billy on their tall horses, cantering down across the pasture. They were headed straight for the pig pen.

Escape was cut off; there was no time for changing into any of the disguises. But there was one chance and Freddy took it. There was a wig of black hair that reached to his shoulders, and there was a thin rattail moustache; he had bought them earlier in the year to disguise himself as a Western bad man. He stuck them on hurriedly, pulled his hat over his eyes, and went to the door where he lounged in plain sight against the doorpost.

The Margarines separated and rode up to him, one on each side, covering him with their shotguns. "Keep your hands away from that gun," Mr. Margarine said. "You're under arrest."

Freddy looked up and stroked his long moustache with a fore trotter. "Shucks, pardner," he said lazily, "you want to be careful with them popguns. I could 'a knocked you both out of your saddles with this little old six-gun while you was makin' up your minds to pull the trigger."

The Margarines looked at him doubtfully. This tough-looking character, facing them so boldly, couldn't be Freddy, Mr. Margarine thought. Like most people who are very sure of themselves, he was rather dumb. He said to Billy: "This isn't the pig we're after."

"What's that?" said Freddy sharply. "Don't try none of your smart cracks on the Comanche Kid, friend, if you don't want your ears blowed off."

"No offense," said Mr. Margarine. "We're looking for a pig named Freddy. And that certainly looks like his horse." He pointed to Cy who stood near them.

"Meanin' to imply that it ain't *mine?*" Freddy said, trying to make his voice as menacing as possible. He moved his right hand down towards his gun butt. "Those are fightin' words, mister."

"Don't be so touchy," said Mr. Margarine. "This Freddy rides a buckskin pony, too. Finding you here, where he lives, and wearing the same kind of Western outfit—well, naturally, we thought we'd found him. We've got a warrant for his arrest." And he flashed his deputy's badge.

"You're the law, hey?" said Freddy sourly. "I don't have no truck with the law. I got a score to settle with this here Freddy myself, but I'll settle it in my own way." He patted his holster. "I come all the way from Spavin Creek, Texas, to settle it. Can't no lally gaggin' long-nosed Eastern rhymeslinger compare himself with the Comanche Kid."

"How do you mean—compare himself?" Mr. Margarine asked.

"He said in one of them poetry pieces of his'n that we looked alike," Freddy growled. He tugged angrily at his moustache—tugged so hard that the still wet mucilage he had attached it with gave way and it nearly came off. He pressed it back quickly, pretending to yawn behind his fore trotter.

Mr. Margarine looked at him thoughtfully. "How would you like to take a job with me? Now wait a minute," he said quickly, "before you refuse." He pulled out a copy of the ad that Jinx had shown Freddy and held it out. "I need someone to help me find this pig, and I think you're just the man. And if you've got a score to settle with him, you'll settle it more quickly this way, and you'll be getting a salary from me at the same time."

Freddy thought a minute. He didn't see how he was going to get away with it: sooner or later Mr. Margarine was bound to find him out. But he realized that very few detectives have ever had such a case offered to them. To be hired to find himself, to disguise himself from himself in order to follow his own tracks—there was something complicated about it that tickled his sense of fun.

"Detective job, hey?" he said. "And a pig, you say? He ain't got no hair."

"What's that got to do with it?" Mr. Margarine asked.

"I'm the Comanche Kid, friend. You hire me to follow this feller's trail, and you're hirin' me to lift his hair. That's how the Comanche Kid operates."

"You mean you'll scalp him?" Billy asked.

"I don't want you to shoot or scalp him," said Mr. Margarine. "Find him. Bring him in alive. I'll see to the rest of it."

"'Taint my way of doing business," said Freddy with a sneer. "But suit yourself. Generally on a job like this, I get paid by the scalp. No scalp, no pay."

Mr. Margarine brought out a fat pocketbook. "I'll pay you the first week right now."

"Week!" Freddy exclaimed. "It don't take a week for the Comanche Kid to do a little job like this." He walked over to Cy and gathered up the rein and swung into the saddle. "See you around," he said, and cantered off towards the woods.

"You're kind of getting yourself into a spot, aren't you, Freddy?" said Cy.

"Maybe. But I'm glad I don't have to scalp myself to get that money. Oh, I can't get away with being the Comanche Kid. Up there I was standing in the doorway with all that bright sky behind me—he couldn't get a good look at me. But they'd have caught me if I hadn't bluffed them."

"What are you going to do about that rattler?" Cy asked.

Freddy said: "Darn those Margarines. All that work we had catching him, and they had to let him out. I wish I'd turned him over to Whibley."

"You ought to have taken him down to that dentist in Centerboro and had his fangs pulled."

"I understand they just grow back in again," said Freddy. "Anyway, he'd scare everybody to death rattling even if he didn't have any fangs. H'm, that's an idea. Wonder if the rabbits could handle it."

He rode up to the Grimby House and had a long talk with the Horribles, and with Georgie and Charles, and having warned them to keep a sharp eye out for the escaped rattler, he circled around to the north and came down out of the woods on to the Margarine farm.

The sun had set; it was dark and beginning to get chilly. As he came down towards the Margarine house he saw lights in the dining room; evidently the family was still at dinner. He rode around to the front of the house and up to the front door and banged on it with the butt of his pistol.

A maid in a little white apron opened the door, saw Freddy, gave a screech and slammed it shut again.

So Freddy banged on it harder.

There were voices calling inside and a bustle of movement, and then the door opened again and Mr. Margarine stood there with a shotgun in his hands. Behind him was Billy and a man in a chauffeur's cap.

"Oh, it's you," he said. "What do you mean, making such a disturbance?"

"If you want that pig," Freddy drawled, "stop yapping at me and go saddle your horse."

"You mean you've found him?"

"I know where he is," Freddy said.

Five minutes later, Mr. Margarine and Billy followed Freddy down the drive. He led them at a trot up along the wall to the Big Woods, then turned in among the trees. Here Freddy said they must leave the horses and proceed on foot.

From this side there was no path to the Grimby house. Though they had flashlights, there were roots to fall over and witch hopple to tangle their feet and low boughs to whip their faces. They stumbled along for a few minutes, then Mr. Margarine stopped.

"This is all nonsense," he said angrily. "I'm paying you to catch this Freddy, not to break my neck looking for him. What is this place?"

"The Big Woods," said Freddy. "Some folks call it Snakeville, on account of the rattlers."

"Say, Dad," said Billy, "That was a rattlesnake in the pig pen this afternoon, wasn't it?"

"You mean there are rattlers in here?" Mr. Margarine demanded.

"So I've heard tell. If you're skeered, better go back," said Freddy contemptuously.

Mr. Margarine hesitated, but Billy said: "We aren't afraid. Go on." And they went.

A minute or two later they came out in an open space. The Grimby house was a black and ominous shadow on the far side of the clearing. "There's his hideout," said Freddy. "You and the boy watch this side. I'll go to the back and drive him out." He stepped towards the house, then jumped aside as a whirring rattle sounded almost under his feet.

"What was that?" said Mr. Margarine.

Before Freddy could answer, another rattle came from behind them.

"Seems to be some of the varmints around tonight," said Freddy calmly. "Just move slow; likely they won't bother us. If you do get bit—" He stopped as the same dry whirr came from several places in the coarse grass around them. Mr. Margarine gasped, and Freddy grinned under his rattail moustache. Those whirrs didn't really sound like rattlesnakes, but it was probably the best the Horribles could do in the short time given them. They were shaking pebbles and hickory nuts in paper bags and a few little boxes that Freddy had noticed in the Grimby attic.

"Rattlesnake bites ain't necessarily fatal," Freddy went on. "You swell up and yell a powerful lot, but—" A high thin screech cut him short. "Huh, one of 'em caught a rabbit," he said. "Well, shucks, in my time I've waded in rattlesnakes up to my hips, and—"

"You go ahead and wade in them," said Mr. Margarine, as a dozen rattles sounded all around them. Come, Billy." One rabbit—Freddy found

Freddy jumped aside as a whirring rattle sounded almost under his feet.

out later it was No. 32 and gave him a bonus for it—managed to hiss. That finished the Margarines. They broke and ran. They stumbled and fell, and got up and ran on, bumping into trees, tangling themselves and tearing their clothes on blackberry bushes. Just before reaching the horses Mr. Margarine got into an argument with a patch of thorn brush. He got away finally, but left most of his riding breeches with his antagonist. And then they found their horses and went pounding back down towards home and safety.

"O K, Brother Horribles," said Freddy. "My best thanks to you. Come in and go to bed now. I guess the Margarine boys won't be hanging around this place much from now on."

Chapter 11

When Freddy had left the mice to go out and talk to Mr. Margarine, he had left the pig pen door open. These four mice were physically fine specimens of their race; they were much more athletic than most mice, who are content to run along baseboards and gobble up crumbs; they had even tried to organize a mouse basketball team, with a field mouse named Howard as the fifth, and baskets made of paper cups tacked up by Mr. Bean, but they couldn't get any games.

Mice on neighboring farms were just too lazy. But powerful as they were, no four mice are big enough to shove a door shut. They pulled and tugged and puffed and panted, but the door stayed open.

They wanted to stay and keep an eye on things for Freddy, but with the door open, if the snake decided to come back before Freddy did—well, four mice are just a gulp and a swallow for a rattler. "We'd better beat it back to the house," said Eek.

They had got about halfway when there was a rustle in the grass ahead of them, and then suddenly a flat head with little beady eyes reared up on a long neck and swayed there in front of them, cutting them off from the barnyard.

"Well, *well!*" whispered the rattlesnake mockingly. "How thoughtful of you to bring me my supper!"

They huddled together, too scared to run. Their eyes followed the flat head as it swung from side to side. But Cousin Augustus, glancing for a second beyond the snake, saw a ripple of movement in the tops of the long grasses. Something was creeping towards them. Of course, maybe it was another rattler. But more likely it was Sniffy Wilson or perhaps John, coming to their rescue. Now if he could just gain a little time, stall the snake off and keep him interested—"Look, snake," he said, "Do you like rabbits?"

"You wouldn't be trying to take my mind off mice, would you?" said the snake with a coarse hissing laugh. "Because that will be a lot easier to do after I've had supper. Only of course you won't be there, will you?"

The other mice moaned, but Cousin Augustus, although he was so scared that even the tip of his tail trembled, said boldly, "Certainly we're trying to. We're offering to tell you where there's a nice fat rabbit. If you'll let us go, that is. Which do you want for supper, four skinny mice or the rabbit? Full of vitamins, rabbits are."

"We-l-l-l," said the snake thoughtfully. Cousin Augustus knew what he was thinking. No rattler ever keeps his word to anybody, and if he promised to let them go, he was thinking that if he could get the rabbit, he would have the mice for dessert. "Sure, I'll make a deal with you," he said.

But before Cousin Augustus could make up

a reply, something brown and white and yellow exploded into action behind the snake. A big paw went smack! against one side of his head, and before he could turn—smack! went a paw against the other side, and then claws dug into his back. He thrashed about, got free, coiled, and struck, as the cat—for it was Arthur—jumped clear.

"Run, my little friends," said Arthur in his most sanctimonious voice as he dodged the sharp fangs, and followed the snake's recovery with a pounce and a hard left and right that must have jarred the rattler to the tip of his tail.

The mice didn't run. They were too anxious to see the end of the fight, and, suspicious as they had been of Arthur, their suspicions had suddenly vanished. The fight didn't end however as they had hoped. Seeing that striking at the cat was useless, the snake uncoiled, brought his tail around with a quick hard slap at Arthur's side, then while Arthur was backing off to get his wind, he wriggled away swiftly through the grass.

Arthur accompanied the mice down to the house. He accepted their thanks with his usual saintly air. "It was nothing, nothing," he said.

"Perhaps my deed will in some slight measure make up for all the wrongs that mice have suffered at the paws of cats. I am genuinely happy to have been of service."

"It just goes to show," said Eeny when they were safe in their cigar box again under the stove, "that people aren't like you think they are. Well, I mean, you can't judge 'em by the way they talk. All this noble stuff about the dear little mouse-friends, stuff that makes you kind of sick—well, he really means it. He means it so much that he'll fight a dangerous snake for it. I don't get it."

"I guess," said Quik, "that people really mean a lot more of what they say than other people think they do."

So they left it at that.

Late that night Freddy was asleep on the pile of sacks in the attic of the Grimby house. Freddy sounded very comfortable. He breathed in little contented puffs, as if he was thinking: "Oh boy, is this nice! Golly, how good it is to snuggle into these nice soft burlap bags!" But some time after midnight he awoke with a yelp. He sat up straight, fighting to wake up the parts of his mind that were still asleep. For something had happened. Something had fallen on the floor beside him with a faint rattle.

But suddenly Old Whibley's deep voice reassured him. The owl was perched on the windowsill. "There, my old Injun fighter; there's a trophy for you. 'Tisn't a scalp for it came off the other end, but it's just as good."

Freddy felt around in the dark and found it. Rattles, six rattles off a rattlesnake's tail.

"Gee whiz, Whibley, did you really catch him?" he said.

The owl didn't answer the question. "I got to worrying about you tonight," he said. "You being naturally low on intelligence, and having further slowed down your wits by eating seven or eight full meals a day, I got to wondering if you'd have the sense to take off that wig and moustache before going to bed."

"Take 'em off?" said Freddy. "Why should I?"

"Good thing I woke you," Whibley said. "Puffing and snorting like a heavy tank crossing a ditch. Give one of these gasps and draw that wig down your throat, and you'd choke to death in two minutes."

"I was not puffing and snorting!" said Freddy

The owl was perched on the window sill.

indignantly. He didn't like any more than you or I would to be told that he snored. "You never mind my wig. Tell me about the rattler."

Old Whibley spread his wings. "Nothing to tell. He's gone to a better land. I may say I have assisted him to a position where he gives great satisfaction." He floated off with a hoot of laughter.

"Ate him, I suppose," said Freddy to himself. "Snakes!" he shuddered. "And he complains about *my* eating habits!" He lay down and pulled the sacks over him.

But he couldn't get to sleep. He knew that the danger Whibley had pretended to find in sleeping with the wig on was all nonsense. The owl had been kidding him. But just the same he couldn't get the wig out of his thoughts. Suppose he drew in a deep breath and the wig did get drawn down his throat. Finally he sat up and took off the wig and moustache and laid them down beside his bed.

But even then he couldn't rest. If he rolled over in his sleep and got close to the wig and if he breathed in hard. . . . He got up and hung the wig and moustache on a nail on the other side of the attic.

It was nearly daylight when he woke again. Charles woke him this time. Perched on the roof he was crowing for all he was worth. Freddy bounded out of his sacks and stuck his head out of the window. "Shut up, will you, you idiot?" he shouted. "Don't you realize that you're an outlaw—that the sheriff is after you? What's the idea of getting up there and announcing to everybody within five miles that this is where you're hiding out?"

"It is my custom," said Charles with dignity, "each day to salute the morn with the appropriate musical notes. It is also my right and my duty. No sheriff or other minion of the law is going to prevent me." And he crowed again.

Freddy went back and got his water pistol. By leaning well out, he could just see Charles, perched on the rooftree above him. He waited until the rooster took a deep breath and pointed his beak at the sky, and then he let him have it. There was a squawk, a thump and a sort of slithering flutter, and Charles, soaking wet and mad as a hornet, was getting up off the ground under the window.

Freddy closed the window, and prudently went over and bolted the attic door. Charles and his big talk was a joke among the animals, but when he was really angry there was nothing funny about it. He had once attacked a Mr. Garble and chased him out of his office and half-way up Main Street in Centerboro.

Charles stamped around for a while, calling Freddy all the names he could think of. But as Freddy didn't answer, he got tired of it after a while, and wandered off grumbling into the woods. Freddy put his wig on then and came down and saddled Cy and rode off in search of adventure. He met it at the first open field he crossed.

Chapter 12

The animals around in the neighborhood had heard what a good effect being laughed at had on Billy Margarine, and as he rode around the countryside they certainly gave him the full treatment. Cows and horses grazing in the fields lifted up their heads and haw-haw'd when he went by, and every tree seemed to be full of giggling birds and chuckling squirrels, and if he stopped beside a stone wall, from inside it came snickers and squeaks of amusement. Even in his bed at night he couldn't get away from it, for Uncle Solomon, the screech owl, had got in the habit of sitting in the woodbine outside Billy's window, and his crazy laughter ran through the boy's troubled dreams.

At first Billy had been pretty mad. He threw stones at the animals, but he realized that that didn't get him anywhere. Even being mad didn't get him anywhere, for they never got mad back—they just laughed harder. He lived in a bigger house and had more expensive clothes than any of the neighboring farmers, who went around in patched overalls and muddy boots. But the animals didn't laugh at them. He couldn't understand it.

Lots of boys who had been brought up like Billy, to have everything he asked for, and to look down on people who didn't have much money, would have left it at that. But Billy thought about it. And pretty soon he began to see that his money and his thoroughbred horse and his fine clothes didn't mean a thing to the animals, or to Mr. and Mrs. Bean either. And when he wondered why they didn't, it came to him that it was because they liked people for what they were, not for what they had.

This was a surprising thought to Billy. He had always pretended that he didn't care whether people liked him or not. Of course he did care, because everybody does. But he had believed that to make people like him he must impress them with how rich and important he was. Now he began to wonder. And he was wondering that morning as he rode up across lots after breakfast, when at the edge of the woods he ran into Freddy, who that morning, of course, was the Comanche Kid.

They both pulled up and looked at each other, and then Freddy said: "If you and your pa hadn't been so scairt we'd have had that pig in the jailhouse this morning."

"All right, so we were scared," said Billy. "What of it?" He looked at the guitar which Freddy had slung across his back. "You play that thing?"

"Sure." Freddy started to unsling the guitar, then stopped. If he took off his gauntlets to pluck the strings, Billy would see that he had trotters instead of hands, and would know he was a pig. "When we're ridin' herd, we play and sing to the cattle. Specially when it's building up for a storm. Keeps 'em from stampeding."

Something giggled in a tree overhead, and a voice said: "They must be deaf. I've heard you sing and it *made* me stampede."

"They laugh at you, too, don't they?" said Billy.

"Squirrels!" said Freddy contemptuously. "They ain't got no manners." He pulled out his pistol. "Where is he?"

"Oh, don't shoot him!" Billy exclaimed. And as Freddy stared: "Well, I mean, he didn't do anything but laugh."

Freddy shot the gun back into the holster. Maybe, he thought, Billy wasn't so bad after all. "O K," he said. "But it ain't healthy to laugh at the Comanche Kid. There's a hospital out where I come from, just built special to take care of folks that laugh at me."

Billy looked at him doubtfully. "Well," he said, "they laugh at me too. All the animals, they just roar whenever they see me. I guess they don't like me." He gave a laugh which he tried to make sound careless. "As if I cared!"

"If you didn't care you wouldn't talk about

it," said Freddy. "But why should they like you? The way I heerd it, you come pushin' in here, snootin' at the Beans because they ain't got much money, pointing your finger and laughing at the animals. They just give you the same treatment. And so you don't like it!" He gave a snort of contempt. "You're a fool, boy!"

To Freddy's surprise, Billy didn't flare up. "Maybe I hadn't ought to have laughed at that pig," he said. "He's sort of the boss animal on the farm, I guess."

"Oh, I wouldn't say he was the boss," said Freddy modestly. "He's smarter than some of the others, I suppose. Quite a poet, too; he swings a mean rhyme."

Billy looked at him in surprise. "I thought you came up here to shoot him?" he said.

Freddy had forgotten for the moment that, as the Comanche Kid, he was out after his own scalp. "That's what I'm aimin' to do, pardner," he said. "But effen he was just an ordinary pig, wouldn't be no glory in shootin' him. Folks the Comanche Kid plugs has got to be important folks—cattle rustlers or bank presidents or such. This here pig now—he's a poet and a bank president and a detective and I don't know what all.

He'll rate a good deep notch on this old six-gun."

"My father's a bank president," said Billy proudly.

"Is that right?" said Freddy. "Better scalp than the pig's," he added thoughtfully. "Twould mount nice. Maybe after I get the pig I could pick a fight with him."

Billy looked at him doubtfully. "You wouldn't do that! Aw, you're kidding me. I don't believe you'll even shoot that Freddy. Anyway, my father doesn't want you to; he just wants to capture him."

Freddy shook his head. "Like to oblige him, but I'm getting out of practise—ain't shot anybody in a week. Last feller was Snake Peters; he jumped my minin' claim in Grisly Gulch— him and Snaggle-tooth Charlie, and a greaser they called Old Nasty. Well, sir, they was holed up in my cabin by the mine shaft . . ."

He continued the story as they rode along. Billy listened eagerly, and when Freddy reached the point where, with one cartridge left in his gun, he had had to get the three claim jumpers in a line so as to drill them all with the single bullet, the boy nearly fell out of the saddle with excitement. "Golly, that's a good story!" he exclaimed.

So Freddy started another one, about the time he was captured by the Pawnees.

At noon they were sitting in the grass up by the edge of the woods, and Freddy was just finishing the tenth chapter of the personal reminiscences of the Comanche Kid, which had to do with a duel he had fought with Geronimo, the Apache chief, when he saw Rabbit No. 23 sitting on a rock a little way off and trying to attract his attention by waving his ears.

Freddy motioned him to approach. "If you got something to say to the Comanche Kid, stranger," he said, "don't stand there wagglin' your ears; come and say it. Message from that pig, I suppose. Offer of surrender, hey?"

No. 23 was a smart rabbit. He gave a quick glance at Billy; then he said: "No, sir. I was just to tell you—you know Mr. Margarine has warned all the Bean animals off his place. Well, this morning he caught one of the cows. He *claims* she was on his side of the fence. Anyway, he caught her and tied her up in his stable, and he says that if you—that is, if that pig, doesn't give himself up within twenty-four hours, he's going to shoot her."

Freddy got up. "Which cow did he catch? And does Mr. Bean know about this?"

"Mrs. Wiggins. No sir, Mr. Margarine said he'd leave Mr. Bean out of it; it was up to Mrs. Wiggins' friends to turn Freddy in. Or if Freddy was such a good friend of hers he'd give himself up."

"I see," said Freddy thoughtfully. "I don't think he'd shoot Mrs. Wiggins—"

"Oh, but he would!" Billy interrupted. "You don't know my dad. He's awful mad at those animals. Wanted to shoot some of them the other day—he said old Bean would probably sue him, but he's got plenty of money to pay if the judge fined him." He paused and frowned unhappily. "I wish he wouldn't," he said. "I don't like those animals any better than he does, and I'd like to get even with them, but not shoot them."

"Kind of a mean man, your pa, ain't he?" said Freddy.

"It isn't that so much," Billy said. "But he gets mad and says he's going to do something,

He saw rabbit No. 23 sitting on a rock waving his ears.

and then he has to do it. He says a bank president, if he gives his word, he has to keep it right to the letter. So even if he knows, when he gets over being mad, that he hadn't ought to carry out some threat he made, he has to do it just the same. He says sometimes he regrets he has such an awful temper."

"He's going to regret it more and more as time goes on," said Freddy, getting to his feet. "Attention, No. 23!" he said to the rabbit.

No. 23 saluted. "Yes, sir."

"Go down and tell the animals not to say anything to Mr. Bean about this. I'll take care of Mrs. Wiggins. And ask everybody to come up to the Grimby house this afternoon; we may have to stand a siege."

Billy had been looking more and more alarmed as Freddy talked, and all at once he jumped up and ran to his horse. But as he put his foot into the stirrup, Freddy's gun snapped out and was leveled at him. "Hold it!" the pig commanded.

"Ah, you wouldn't shoot!" Billy said, and swung into the saddle. "Comanche Kid, hey?" And he yelled with laughter. "The Comanche Pig! Boy, will Dad be sore when he hears how you fooled him!" He galloped off towards home.

Freddy didn't bother to shoot one of his blanks; he just stood staring after the boy until Cy ranged up alongside him. "Well, come on, pig, come on!" the horse said. "Get after him."

"We can't catch him," said Freddy.

"We can have a darned good try," Cy said. "You've got that rope on the saddle horn, haven't you? Get on!"

So Freddy unslung his guitar, dropped it on the grass and jumped into the saddle. He took his rope from the horn, and as Cy stretched out at full speed he began whirling the loop around his head. "Yippeee!" he yelled.

Billy's horse was a tall, rangy hunter, and there seemed little chance that Cy could overtake him. But to get down to the Margarine place they had to cross several very rough and rocky pastures, and the hunter was taking no chances of breaking a leg. He ran, but he didn't run as fast as Cy, who tore recklessly along, leaping boulders and crashing through bushes. And halfway across the second field Freddy caught up. The rope circled and the loop fell neatly over Billy's head.

"Stop!" Freddy yelled. "Or I'll yank you out

of the saddle!" And Billy pulled up, as the noose was drawn gently tight just above his elbows.

"O K," said Billy. O K, I give in. What do we do now?"

Chapter 13

Mrs. Wiggins wasn't much of a worrier. After her capture by Mr. Margarine and his stable man, Thomas, she was locked into one of a row of box stalls where the horses lived. She munched on the forkful of hay that Thomas had thrown into the stall. "If they're going to shoot me," she said to herself, "they're going to shoot me, and I might as well get all I can out of them." And she thought with pleasure of the kick she had got home on Mr. Mar-

garine's shin, after they had sneaked up and
slipped a rope around her neck, and were dragging her down to the barn.

Perhaps she might have worried more if she
hadn't been sure that Freddy would hear about
her capture. She had seen Mrs. Pomeroy sitting
on the roof when she had been led into the
stall. The robin had waved a claw, and then
had flown off towards home. Pretty soon, she
thought, Freddy would come to the rescue, riding, like a knight in shining armor, with a pistol
in each hand, and Jinx and Bill and Hank and
the rest of the animals at his back. It was a pretty
confused picture Mrs. Wiggins painted in her
mind, but the main fact about it was clear: Freddy would certainly come.

About noon Mr. Margarine reappeared. He
opened the upper half of the stall door and said:
"I suppose you can talk, like all the rest of
Bean's menagerie?"

Mrs. Wiggins was one of those rare people
who, when they don't have anything to say,
don't say it. She went on munching hay.

"It doesn't matter," Mr. Margarine said. "I
have sent a note over to Beans, stating my terms.
Either the pig gives himself up, or you will be

shot. I have nothing against you personally, you understand; I am—" He broke off as a voice some distance away began calling.

"Come Sweetie! *Sweetie Pie!* Come kitty, kitty, kitty!" It was Mrs. Margarine. She came inside, still calling, and then saw her husband. "Oh, there you are, Elihu. I can't think what has become of that cat. I haven't seen him for several days. Why, what's the matter with the cow?"

"She's coughing. I suppose she choked on the hay."

But Mr. Margarine was wrong about that as he was about so many things. Mrs. Wiggins wasn't coughing. She was trying not to laugh out loud at the thought of the saintly and dignified Sweetie Pie.

There are very few cows, or people either, who would feel any inclination to laugh under such circumstances. Freddy would organize a rescue, but would he organize it in time? If he didn't, she would be led out in the cold dawn to face a firing squad. But there's no sense in crossing a bridge until you come to it. That's what Mrs. Wiggins thought. So she went on enjoying her laugh. And it was then that she got her idea. She stopped laughing and began to think.

"Oh, here," said Mrs. Margarine. "Here's a package that came for you, Elihu."

Mr. Margarine took it. "Where's it from?"

"It was left on the porch," she said. "Look, there's some writing on it."

Mr. Margarine read it. *"Enclosed find one scalp, formerly attached to your hired man, the Comanche Kid. Compliments of Freddy, the Terror of the Plains.* p. s. *I'll send you Billy's scalp next."* He tore the paper off and pulled out a hank of long black hair, at which Mrs. Margarine began to scream.

Her husband snapped at her. "Be quiet. Can't you see that this is a wig? That man I hired—he wore it. He was no Westerner—he was the pig!" Mr. Margarine was so mad at having been fooled that he turned white, and his lips were pressed together in a thin line. "I'll— if it's the last thing I do, I'll—" He stopped suddenly and the wig and the paper dropped from his hands. "Billy!" he exclaimed. "Where's Billy?" He turned and limped towards the house, shouting for Thomas, and for Jenks, the chauffeur.

Mrs. Margarine was a tall woman with a long face. If she had looked out of a barn window at you in a dim light, you might have thought she was one of her own thoroughbreds. She picked up the wig and looked at it in a puzzled way, then hung it over the lower door of the stall. "Well really!" she said out loud. "That's not Billy's hair. Why is Elihu so disturbed?" She was not a very bright woman.

Mrs. Wiggins could no longer control her laughter. Partly it was relief at the assurance that her friends were really on the job. For she guessed that the threat about Billy meant that Freddy had captured the boy. But mostly she laughed because by sending the wig Freddy had made a monkey out of Mr. Margarine. He really had disposed of Mr. Margarine's hired gunman and had sent in his scalp as a proof and a warning.

When Mrs. Wiggins really got to laughing she unsettled the entire neighborhood. She roared so that a thunderstorm could come up and go crashing and banging across the sky and you would never hear it. Rabbits on distant hillsides crouched trembling in the grass, and mice and squirrels and chipmunks covered their ears with their paws. "Oh, ho, ho!" Mrs. Wiggins shouted, and Mrs. Margarine cried out in dismay and turned and ran for the house. "O, ho, hoo, *haw!*" Mrs. Wiggins roared. Only of course there aren't enough letters in the alphabet to spell what that laugh sounded like.

Up at the Grimby house in the Big Woods, Freddy heard it, and he grinned at his captive, who was sitting on a pile of sacks in the attic, guarded by Robert and Georgie. "That's my partner, Mrs. Wiggins, you hear," he said. "She's laughing. But of course hearing a cow laugh is no novelty to you, is it?"

"She hasn't got much to laugh about," said Billy sullenly.

"Oh, I don't know," said Jinx, who was sitting on the windowsill. "She's got your old man; he's good for about a laugh a minute. Shucks, he don't even have to open his mouth—just looking at him gives 'em the screaming giggles."

"Aw, lay off me, will you?" said the boy. "You wouldn't be so funny if you didn't have me locked up here."

"I guess maybe you're right," Freddy said.

"O, ho, hoo, haw!" Mrs. Wiggins roared.

"It isn't very nice to tease prisoners. Well, you won't be a prisoner long. Your father will start looking for you as soon as he gets the Comanche Kid's scalp. We'll let him worry for an hour or two, and then we'll make him a proposition. You'll be home by suppertime."

"You don't know my dad," said Billy. "He said if you didn't give yourself up he'd shoot the cow, and he means just that. No matter what you do to me. But I don't suppose he thinks you'd dare do anything to me."

"To tell you the truth, we wouldn't do anything to you," Freddy said. "But he can't be sure of that."

"He'll shoot the cow just the same," said Billy, "because he said he would."

Jinx snarled angrily. "You're a fine lot, you Margarines," he said. "You come into a peaceful neighborhood and try to run things and push everybody around and get everybody mad and worried and upset—and now you want to start shooting them! Let me tell you something, you stuck-up little squinch: if your father shoots Mrs. Wiggins, or any other friend of ours—"

"I don't *want* him to shoot her!" Billy interrupted, almost tearfully. "But what can I do about it? Look, you've made fun of me a lot—well, I've made fun of you, too: so that makes us even, doesn't it? I'd like to live here and be friends with everybody. It isn't any fun riding around when you know every animal you see hates you."

"We don't hate you," Freddy said. "We just don't think . . . that is, we think it's sort of silly, your going around pretending to be so much better than everybody else, just because you have a pocket full of money, and a fine horse and shiny expensive riding boots—"

"I don't like these boots," Billy said. "I'd like to have Western boots like yours. And a ten-gallon hat and a gun belt—"

"Wait a minute," said Freddy. "Let me think." He looked thoughtfully at the boy. "Are you as good at keeping your word as your father is?" And when Billy said yes, he hoped he was, Freddy said: "All right, I'm going to believe you. I'm going to try an experiment. You're about my size. Now by this time your father must know that we've captured you, and he'll come right here. We'll fight him if we have to, but it will be better if we don't. So we'll go down to my place and I'll fit you out with a complete cowboy outfit. Only you'll have to give me your word you'll stay with me and not try to escape."

"All right," said Billy. "I promise. Only if we should meet my Dad—"

"We won't meet him. He'll probably guess that we're holding you here, and he'll come into the Big Woods from your side, the west side. You and I will ride out the east side and circle around down to the farm. Jinx, you and the other animals better scatter and go home. We can't stand a siege here, because Mr. Margarine and his men will certainly be armed."

"And how about me?" Charles said angrily. "I can't go back; I'll be arrested. If they come search the henhouse the way they did the pig pen—"

"Oh, don't be so scared," said Jinx. "What could they do with you if they did arrest you? Who'd want a stringy old rooster—"

"I'm *not* scared!" Charles shouted. "Let old Margarine come. Let him bring on his armed cohorts, let him put guns in the hands of his greasy scullions and lead them against me. Scared?" He thumped his chest with a claw. "Let the odds be what they may—a hundred, a thousand, a million to one; this proud rooster heart—"

"Is just a giblet," said Freddy sharply. "Dry up; there's no time for an oration now. You can hide in the spruces back of the house; nobody will find you there if you keep your noisy beak shut. Come on, Billy."

While all this was going on at the Grimby house, Mr. J. J. Pomeroy was talking to Mrs. Wiggins. He had flown up to see how she was getting along in her prison, and to see what chances there were of helping her to escape.

When he had dropped down from the sky above the Margarine place and perched on a fence post to look things over, he had been able to see straight into the door of her stall. And what he saw startled him so that he nearly fell off the post. It was a broad pale face, over which straggled long locks of lank black hair. And as he started, it broke into song.

> *"Freddy the pig*
> *Has lost his wig,*
> *   And he's also lost his Wiggins,*
> *Leave 'em alone*
> *And they'll come home—*

"How will I finish that, J. J.?" it called.

"Good gracious!" he exclaimed. "Mrs. Wiggins! I see; that's Freddy's wig, isn't it? . . . Well, now, how's this?

> *"Freddy the pig*
>   *Has lost his wig.*
>   *And his Wiggins too, he's lost.*
>   *Leave 'em alone*
>   *And they'll come home—*

"H'm. Bossed, frost . . . Oh—at almost no extra cost. How's that?"

"It's pretty, but what does it mean?" Mrs. Wiggins asked.

"Let's think about that later. Now I have to go back and report. How's everything? Anything new?"

"As a matter of fact, there is," said the cow. "I've had an idea."

"Bless me!" said Mr. Pomeroy admiringly.

"You may well say 'Bless me!' " replied Mrs. Wiggins. "Now, look here. Can you mew?"

"Mew?" he said. "Me? No. I can chirp, I can warble. But mew—no. However, there's a catbird, a Mr. Johnson or Puddleford or some such name, down the road. He's a good mewer. Why?"

"There's nobody in the house but Mrs. Margarine and two maids," Mrs. Wiggins said. "The men have gone to look for Billy. Mrs. M. was out here calling for Arthur a while ago. She wants to find him. Now you see, if you could mew, you could pretend to be Arthur and lead her and the maids away; and then, with nobody here to stop you, all the animals could come over and get me out of this place."

"If you want mewing, why not get a cat?" said the robin.

"Gracious, I never thought of that!" said the cow. "Where's Jinx?"

"Why not get Arthur?" said Mr. Pomeroy. "He's a good guy."

"Arthur'd be embarrassed," she said. "Mrs. Margarine's name for him . . . well, he'd just be sick if all the animals heard what it is. Oh dear, even if Jinx does the mewing they'll hear it, because they'll have to be here. No, let's just forget the whole thing."

Mr. Pomeroy started to protest, but he knew that the cow was too kind-hearted to give in; she wouldn't hurt Arthur's feelings. "O K," he said. "I guess you'll be out of here soon enough, anyway." And he said goodbye and went. But he went straight down to see Arthur.

The big tortoise-shell cat looked unhappy. "I wish we could think of some other way," he said. "I won't be able to look any of you animals in the eye without blushing, if you know that name. But if it's Mrs. Wiggins' safety—yes, of course I'll do it. I have to. If I didn't, I couldn't look any of you in the eye at all, blush or no blush. Come on."

The other animals were coming back from the Grimby house. Mr. Pomeroy told them the plan, and they started at once for the Margarine place. The Horribles had come back too, and they went along.

Mrs. Margarine had stationed the maids at the back windows to keep an eye on the stables, in case of an attempted rescue. Suddenly one of them gave a screech. "Oh, Mis' Margarine! Your Sweetie! He just went around the corner of the garage!"

Mrs. Margarine dashed out into the kitchen. "Come Nellie! Martha, you stay on guard." She rushed out of the back door.

There was an open space back of the house

around which stood the barn, the stables, and other buildings. Arthur didn't show himself again—as a matter of fact he had gone some distance up towards the Big Woods. He sat behind a bush and said softly, "Merowp! Merowp" very short, so that it was hard to tell where the sound came from.

"Co-o-o-me, Kitty kitty! Co-o-o-me, Sweetie Pie!" Mrs. Margarine called, and went towards it, with Nellie beside her.

"Merowp!" Arthur stepped into view, walking very dignified as if he didn't see her, as cats do. Then he went behind another bush a little farther away.

This went on for some time. Before she knew it, Mrs. Margarine was on the edge of the woods and nearly a quarter of a mile from the house.

"We ought to go back, ma'am," said Nellie fearfully. "Then rattlesnakes—"

"Pooh!" said Mrs. Margarine. "Don't be silly!" And she went in among the deep shadows of the big trees.

As soon as she disappeared the rescue party made a dash for the stable. Martha saw them and rushed out; but rushed right back in again with Mrs. Wogus galloping after her. Mrs.

Wogus chased her through the kitchen and the dining room and the hall and halfway up the front stairs. But cows aren't used to stairs. Mrs. Wogus backed down, and then stood guard in the hall.

Outside, the rescue party wasn't getting anywhere. The upper half of the stall door was open, but the lower half was padlocked, and too high for Mrs. Wiggins to climb over. Hank backed up to it and tried to kick it down with his big iron shoes, but it didn't even shake, and Hank stopped. He said it jarred him so it made his teeth ache. In the kennel the hounds made quite a fuss, but they couldn't get out.

The dogs found some boxes and tried to get Mrs. Wiggins to climb over, but when she stepped on them the boxes caved in, and finally she said she'd rather be shot than try again.

The Horribles had stood around watching; they were too small to be of any help. But they had all been thinking. They did quite a lot of thinking, on and off; mostly ordinary rabbit thoughts, about which garden had the tenderest lettuce and the best way of dodging hawks. But they also thought a lot about who they could scare next with their war dance. And pretty soon all their noses were turned towards the Big Woods. Then 18 looked at 23, and 23 nudged 7, and 7 whispered in 38's ear, and all at once all twenty-five of them started for the woods. Their little white tails bounced up and down. It looked as if someone had thrown several handfuls of small white rubber balls, which went bounding along across the fields till they disappeared among the trees.

Chapter 14

There were a lot of things going on all at once.
Freddy and Billy were riding down the eastern
side of the woods towards the pig pen, and Mr.
Margarine and his two men, with shotguns held
at the ready, were creeping up on the Grimby
house, and Mrs. Wogus was sitting in Mr. Margarine's front hall, admiring herself in the big
hall mirror, and Mrs. Margarine was being
silently surrounded by the Horrible Thirty, as

she went farther and farther into the woods, calling: "Here, Sweetie! Come kitty-pie! Come spitty—spitty—spitty!" For her tongue was tired, she had called so many times, and it kept saying the words wrong.

It is always a little scary going from the warm sunshine of the fields into the cool gloom of the woods. Nellie had fallen behind and at last turned quietly back, and Mrs. Margarine went on slowly. And then all at once, in a particularly gloomy spot, the Horribles jumped out from behind tree trunks and bushes and went into their dance.

Mrs. Margarine gave a loud screech, and then one that was not quite so loud, and then one that was just a sort of moan, and she dashed from side to side of the prancing circle, but didn't dare to try to break through when she saw the knives.

The Horribles paid no attention. They pranced and sang.

"We are the Horrible Thirty,
Red-eyed, bloodthirsty and dirty.
We like to hear our enemies squall,
As we chop 'em fine and we chop 'em small.

We like to hear our enemies squeal,
As we chop 'em up for our evening meal.
We like to see our enemies squinch,
As we chop 'em slowly, inch by inch. . . ."

Mrs. Margarine had sunk down on the ground and covered her face with her hands. The Horribles went on bouncing and singing but they were beginning to get tired. Finally No. 16 said to 23: "Well, what do we do now?"

Usually, if their victim didn't break away from them, they would threaten to come again and chop him to pieces, and then after they had let him go they would have a good laugh together and go off in search of someone else to scare. But it wasn't doing Mrs. Wiggins any good just to scare Mrs. Margarine.

"If Robert and Georgie were here," 23 said, "we could take her somewhere and lock her up."

"Where?" 16 asked. "Mr. Margarine's up at the Grimby house."

"I've got it!" said 23 suddenly. "Go down and get Robert and the rest of them, 16." Then he held up one paw. "Brother Horribles," he shouted, "Look upon the prisoner."

The dance stopped and they crowded around Mrs. Margarine. She peeked through her fingers at them, then shuddered and covered her eyes tighter than ever.

"Brother Horribles," said 23, "guard the prisoner well. If she makes one false move, chop her into small bits. About one inch square." He waved his knife, and the others said: "Yes, Your Dreadfulness," and waved theirs. And Mrs. Margarine shuddered some more.

So 23 went out to meet the other animals. He told them his plan, and they followed him into the woods. They surrounded Mrs. Margarine, and Hank stepped up to her. "Madam," he said politely, "kindly rise and follow me."

Mrs. Margarine took her hands from her face. When, instead of the small queer-looking Horribles, she saw Hank and the dogs and Mrs. Wurzburger—just ordinary farm animals—she gave a great sigh of relief and got up. She followed them without a word back across the fields. In case the maids were looking out of the windows, Georgie ran on ahead and did a lot of barking in front of the house. They led Mrs. Margarine around to the box stall where Mrs. Wiggins was imprisoned. "Climb in if you please Madam," said Hank and gallantly held out a hoof to help her.

"In *here?*" she exclaimed. "I want to go into the house."

"If you please," said Hank firmly, and as she still objected, Robert growled and showed his teeth. She put her hands on the top of the half-door and vaulted lightly in. Then Hank shut the upper half of the door and latched it. "Keep her quiet, Mrs. W.," he said. "We're clearing out now, but we'll be back."

In the front hall Mrs. Wogus had finally begun to get bored. You can admire yourself in a mirror for quite a long time, but after a while it stops being fun. At first you're pretty pleased, and you look at yourself full-face and smile and try different expressions, and then you try to see if maybe your profile isn't pretty noble—but then you begin to notice things that aren't so good. With head thrown back and eyelids half closed, are you really important-looking or just a stuffed shirt? Is that smile really sweet and charming, or is it just sappy? Mrs. Wogus was not a very bright cow, but after all she was a cow, and the more she gazed, the unhappier she got. Finally she shook her head mournfully, turned her back on the mirror and went to the front door.

It was at about this time that Mr. Margarine and his two men rode into the yard, after having explored the Grimby house and found it empty. Without a glance at the closed box stall, he ran around to the front door, and he was just turning the knob when Mrs. Wogus opened it and stuck her head out, almost into his face.

Well, Mr. Margarine was pretty surprised. He had expected to see his wife, not a cow. But before he could say anything, Mrs. Wogus gave him a push that knocked him off the porch, then turned and plunged back through the dining room and kitchen and out the back door. Thomas was leading the horses back to the stable. He gave a yell, but Mrs. Wogus came thundering down on him, horns lowered, and he gave a different kind of yell and ducked into the garage. Mrs. Wogus pounded off towards home.

Now all three sisters—Mrs. Wiggins, Mrs. Wogus and Mrs. Wurzburger—looked a good deal alike. Of course if you knew them well, you could tell them apart. Mrs. Wiggins looked kind and intelligent, Mrs. Wogus looked kind

and dumb, and Mrs. Wurzburger looked kind
and sort of halfway between. But Mr. Margarine really knew them only slightly and he
thought that Mrs. Wogus was Mrs. Wiggins,
and that she had escaped from the stall. Naturally, if she had escaped, it was his wife's fault,
and he went to the foot of the stairs and yelled
for her.

It was nearly half an hour later that having
questioned both Nellie and Martha, he saddled
up again and rode back to the Big Woods to
hunt for his wife.

In the box stall, Mrs. Margarine had been at
first rather frightened. She was not afraid of
cows as a rule, but when she had started to shout
for help, Mrs. Wiggins had threatened her with
her horns. So she sat down on the straw in the
corner and tried to keep out of the cow's way.

But Mrs. Wiggins was a kindly person; after a
few minutes, she said: "You've no call to be
scared. I won't hurt you. Only—no hollering."

"I don't propose to 'holler' as you call it,"
said Mrs. Margarine stiffly. "May I ask what you
expect to gain by this outrageous behavior?"

"Outrageous behavior!" Mrs. Wiggins said.
"That's a funny name for being roped and

Mrs. Wogus stuck her head out.

dragged in here and locked up. Matter of fact, you've had the same treatment, so I might ask what *you* expect to gain."

Mrs. Margarine thought this over. Then she said: "Maybe you're right. We both want to get out. Now just let me call to Thomas or Jenks—"

"No!" said Mrs. Wiggins firmly, and lowered her horns.

For a while neither said anything. Then Mrs. Margarine said: "Oh, dear; really, er— Mrs—"

"Wiggins."

"Mrs. Wiggins, can't we come to some agreement? If I promise to release you, would you let me call for the men?"

"I'd like to, ma'am. But I promised my friends," said the cow.

"In other words, you don't trust me?"

"Why no, ma'am, since you put it that way— I don't."

Mrs. Margarine looked angry; then she laughed. "I daresay you're right. I can hardly imagine myself keeping a promise to a cow."

"A cow or a man—what's the difference," Mrs. Wiggins said. "It's *you* that makes the promise."

Mrs. Margarine thought about this for quite

a while. At last she said: "Do you know, I never thought of that before! And to think it's a cow that set me right. I had no idea that cows . . . Why, dear me; that was very friendly of you."

"I don't feel unfriendly, ma'am," said Mrs. Wiggins. "Only towards Mr. Margarine. You know very well why."

Mrs. Margarine sighed. "Yes, I know. Elihu is so masterful. That red barn of Mr. Bean's—I didn't really care about that at all, but I just mentioned it one day, and he decided that the color must be changed."

"It's not his to change, ma'am."

"Please don't keep calling me ma'am," said Mrs. Margarine. "My name is Mirabel."

"Mirabel Margarine—that's very pretty," said the cow. "But really—"

"Oh, please!" Mrs. Margarine pleaded.

Mrs. Wiggins gave her comfortable laugh. Of course it was her polite laugh; not the great roaring laugh she gave when she was really amused. "Why very well, then—Mirabel," she said.

After that they got on quite well together. And when Mrs. Margarine learned that Mrs. Winfield Church of Centerboro, was a friend of Mrs. Wiggins', she was much impressed. For Mrs. Margarine was a snob and she knew that Mrs. Winfield Church was almost as rich as Mr. Margarine. They talked of this and that, and there was only one interruption, when they heard someone outside—Mrs. Margarine said it was Thomas—say in a low voice: "Sounded like her talkin'—the boss's wife."

"Sounded like a cow to me," said Jenks.

"Better not let the boss hear you say that," said Thomas, and they giggled.

"Anyway," said Thomas, "The cow isn't there. She escaped. So I'm going to open that door and see who's in there."

So he did, and out came Mrs. Margarine and Mrs. Wiggins. The cow didn't stop for any conversation. The two men were so astonished to see again what was apparently the same cow that had just dashed out of the back door, that they let her get a good start before trying to stop her. Then they ran to get horses and a rope; but Mrs. Margarine called them back, and told them to let the cow go.

"But Mr. Margarine wanted to keep her locked up," Thomas protested.

"Are you telling *me* what Mr. Margarine wants?" she demanded.

"No, ma'am," he said. "Only—"

"Only you'll lose your job if you don't keep still," she said sharply, and Thomas backed down.

But Mrs. Margarine looked after the cow, who was trotting over the fields towards home. And when Mrs. Wiggins turned, just before passing out of sight, and smiled at her, with a smile that was so broad on her big face that you could see it plainly even at that distance, Mrs. Margarine took out her handkerchief and waved it.

Like a lot of people, she wasn't so bad at all when you got to know her a little. Many snobs are quite nice people, otherwise.

Chapter 15

While Mr. Margarine and his two men were creeping up on the empty Grimby house—and Charles, sitting in his spruce tree, thought they looked pretty silly at it—Freddy and Billy were down at the pig pen. Billy had put on Freddy's best shirt, the blue one with the yellow lightning flashes on it, and his second best cowboy boots and big hat, and then Freddy had buckled a handsome gun belt around the boy's hips. Freddy's pistols, of course—the water pistol and the regular gun loaded with blanks—he couldn't give up; and there were no other guns available to put into the empty holsters.

"Never mind," Freddy said, "We'll ride down to Centerboro and get you some guns. And a Mexican saddle, too. That little English saddle is all wrong. Oh, sure—and a rope."

Billy was delighted with the outfit, and as they cantered down the road towards town, he talked excitedly about how they could ride together and practice shooting and roping, and the games they could play. "Only Dad," he said thoughtfully—"he maybe won't like it. He thinks this cowboy stuff is silly."

"I don't see that it's any sillier than chasing foxes all over the landscape," said Freddy. "But I expect he won't mind so much—he wants you to have a good time."

Billy said doubtfully that he guessed so.

With his shiny boots and well-cut breeches he seemed to have laid aside all the arrogance and contempt that he had shown towards the animals. Freddy began to think that his experiment was a success.

On the outskirts of town, Freddy pulled up. "You go in to the Busy Bee and buy what you need," he said. "I'd better wait; I don't want to meet the sheriff. Meet you here in an hour."

So Billy rode on. But as he turned into Main Street, a police car cut in ahead of him, and two state troopers jumped out, drew their pistols, and ordered him to pull up.

"Is he the guy, Wes?" one asked.

"Sure," said Wes. "I'd know that shirt anywhere. Get down, pig. You're under arrest."

"Who are you calling 'pig'?" Billy demanded. "You let me alone."

"He wants to know who we're calling 'pig'," said Wes. "That's a good one—hey, Herb?"

"Yeah," said the other trooper. "Come on; get down, pig. You're going to the hoosegow, the jailhouse, the gorilla-hatch."

"But I'm *not* the one you're looking for," Billy protested angrily. "I know him; he's a pig named Freddy." He took off his hat. "Look at me; do I look like a pig?"

"Kind of," said Herb.

"Not exactly," said Wes. "But we know you; you're awful good at disguising yourself. Come on, quit stalling; ride ahead of us over to the jail."

So Billy was taken over to the jail and locked

in a cell by the sheriff, who, when the boy again protested that he was not Freddy, said: "I'll be honest with you, friend. As I remember this Freddy, he was a smart looking feller—brainy, I'd call him. You don't look much like him and that's a fact. But these troopers say you're him. I can't contradict 'em."

Freddy waited for two hours, getting madder and madder all the time. "I ought to have known better than to have taken his word that he wouldn't try to escape," he said.

"Yeah," said Cy, "The great detective kind of laid an egg, didn't he?"

"Just the same," said Freddy, "I still believe he meant to keep his word. I think—well, something must have happened in the Busy Bee— something to delay him. You go around behind that hedge and wait for me. I'm going scouting."

Luckily he had an old raincoat of Mr. Bean's strapped to his saddle. He put this on, punched his hat into a different shape and tilted it over his eyes, and walked on boldly into town.

Nobody paid much attention to him. A lot of funny looking people came to Centerboro in the summertime; he really didn't look any

queerer than some of them. In front of the
Busy Bee he stopped. It would be dangerous to
go in. Mr. Metacarpus, the manager, was always
on the lookout for shoplifters, and Freddy did
not want to become even an innocent object of
suspicion. Luckily he was saved the trouble.

A voice behind him said: "The troopers
picked him up right on Main Street. What a
nerve—coming right into town!"

"Well, I always said that pig was gettin' too
big for his breeches," said another voice.

Freddy didn't even turn to see who was speaking. He knew at once what had happened. He
turned away and walked straight over to the
jail. As he entered the gate a car with two troopers in it swung out and up the street. He went
on into the sheriff's office.

The sheriff was reading a newspaper. He
took his glasses off quickly when Freddy came
in. "Well, sir?" he said.

"I'd like to see that pig that was just arrested," said Freddy. "I represent the F. B. I."

"O. K.," said the sheriff, getting up. "Got any
identification?"

"My papers are in my other coat," said Freddy. "I came over here in a hurry—"

"No matter," said the sheriff. He laughed. "Around these parts, we say that F. B. I. means 'Freddy Bean, Investigator.' He's a detective, you know."

"So I've heard," said Freddy, and he thought: "My goodness, why didn't *I* think of that!"

The sheriff unlocked Billy's cell, let Freddy in, and locked it again. "Holler when you want to get out," he said, and went back to his office.

"I wish all I had to do was holler," said Billy. "My father will be awful mad about this."

"He's awful mad anyway," said Freddy. "So we won't worry about that."

"I mean he'll be mad at me," said the boy. "Being put in jail."

Freddy said: "It's no disgrace being arrested by mistake."

"You don't know my father," said Billy. "I almost got arrested once for riding on the wrong side of the street. Dad said if I had it would have done him a lot of harm. He's president of a bank. He said if I'd been arrested people would have made up awful stories about us, and a lot of people would have stopped doing busi-

ness with his bank. He says he has a lot of enemies who would jump at the chance to pass on
gossip about him."

"Well, he's the kind of man who makes enemies," Freddy said. "I'm president of a bank
myself. I've been in jail twice for things I didn't
do and it didn't hurt my business. But of course
our bank depositors aren't people, they're animals. But that's neither here nor there. I can
get you out of here, I think. But if I do, what
will you do for me?"

"I'll let that cow out—the one that Dad captured," Billy said. Neither of them knew that
Mrs. Wiggins had already escaped.

"Fair enough," said Freddy. "But if I get you
out . . . well, what I was thinking of was hollering for the sheriff, and having you pretend
to be me and walk out in this coat. But that
would put me on a sort of a spot, because your
father—"

"Yes, Dad will want to get even with you—
he'd try to keep you in jail just the same, even
if I told him you helped me to escape. You'll
have to square yourself with him first. I think
maybe if you apologized—"

"Nothing doing," said Freddy firmly. "But

let me think." He didn't really need to think. He knew how to manage Billy's escape, but he wanted first to find out if the boy would play fair with him. And he thought he would. For Billy could easily have pretended that he could get his father to let Freddy off. Instead, he had admitted that he couldn't do anything. Freddy was beginning to like him.

"Well," Freddy said. "I'd better call the sheriff. I've an idea that—" He broke off at the sound of approaching voices.

"Why, it's Dad!" Billy exclaimed. "Oh, golly, if he finds me here—"

"Quick! Get under the cot!" Freddy was already stripping off the raincoat. As Billy scrambled under, the sheriff and Mr. Margarine appeared at the door of the cell to see Freddy seated mournfully on the edge of the cot, staring at the floor.

"Ah," said Mr. Margarine grimly, "You villain, you wretch. Where is my son? What have you done with him?"

"He's safe," Freddy said. "And he's right where I can lay my hand on him any time I want to."

"You scoundrel!" Mr. Margarine exclaimed.

"You wretch! You murderous villain!"

"Look, mister," put in the sheriff mildly. "I don't mind a man callin' names if he's good at it. But you ain't. You keep repeating, like a worn-out talking machine record. If you got a proposition to make, make it. Otherwise, quit disturbing my prisoner."

Mr. Margarine gave him a steely glare. "This —this creature has kidnaped my son, and has threatened to send me his scalp. What do you expect me to do—embrace him?"

He probably wouldn't like it any more than the name calling," said the sheriff. "Look, you want your boy. What'll you do if Freddy turns him loose for you?"

"I suppose you expect me to say that I'll drop my case against him—let him go," Mr. Margarine said. "I will make no such bargain. He wouldn't dare harm a Margarine!"

Freddy looked up. "Tisn't a question of daring. But you're right—I wouldn't harm him. But I might succeed in showing him that his father was a mean, hard man, who cared more about his business reputation than about having his family like him. It wouldn't be hard to prove. Billy has always thought you were fond

Freddy was seated mournfully on the edge of the cot.

of him. Once he sees you care more for kicking
me around than you do for his safety—well,
how's he going to like it?"

Mr. Margarine didn't say anything. He was
mad, but he looked pretty upset too. Then the
sheriff said: "Mr. Margarine, being the sheriff,
I don't want to see any trouble here for either
party. Suppose Freddy produces your boy—will
you drop your case and let him go?"

"How can he produce him if he isn't set free
first?" Mr. Margarine asked. "And do you think
I'd take his word that he'd release the boy?

"Maybe he could send for the boy—have him
brought here." The sheriff turned to Freddy.
"How about it?"

"I'll produce him here," said Freddy with a
wink at the sheriff. "If Mr. Margarine will accept the bargain."

Now Mr. Margarine really did care a lot
about Billy, and so there wasn't much else he
could do but agree. He was pretty sour about it.

So then Freddy said: "O. K., Billy," and the
boy crawled out from under the cot.

Well, Mr. Margarine pretty nearly had a fit,
he was so mad. He didn't stamp and yell, but
he stood perfectly still and he bawled out the

sheriff and he bawled out Freddy and he even bawled out Billy—probably because he was so relieved to find that he was all right. The sheriff pretended to be astonished that Billy was in the cell, but naturally Mr. Margarine didn't believe him. "You'll lose your job for this—I'm telling you straight," he said.

The sheriff was unlocking the cell door. He started to reply, but Billy interrupted him. "Listen, Dad," he said; "you can't do that."

"Oh, but I can," said his father. "I have only to say the word in the right places—"

"If you do, I'll tell everybody I was arrested and locked up in jail," Billy said firmly.

"What?" Mr. Margarine exclaimed. "You wouldn't do that, son. You don't know how people pick up a story like that and repeat it. You don't know what harm it would do."

"I can't help it," said the boy. "The sheriff hasn't done any harm. And neither has Freddy."

His father changed the subject. "Where did you get those frightful clothes? Come home now and get into something decent."

Billy said that he liked the clothes, and that he wanted to get a Western saddle and some boots and things to go with them—a complete cowboy outfit. His father looked distressed, but he said: "Well, if you want them I suppose you'll have to have them." Then he paused. "I'm warning you, pig," he said. "I'm letting you go because I have to. But keep out of my way. I'll shoot you on sight. Come, Billy."

Billy hung back. "I'll let your cow out," he whispered to Freddy. "And I'll meet you in an hour up where I met you this morning." Then he went on after his father.

"I sure was surprised to see that boy in there, Freddy," said the sheriff when they were alone.

"I bet you were," said Freddy with a grin.

"But why did you wait for Margarine?" the sheriff asked. "You know about these window bars."

Freddy did indeed know about the window bars. The sheriff was a kindly man, and once several years ago the prisoners had complained about the bars. They had said that iron bars made them feel shut in, made them nervous. "We have to have bars," the sheriff had said. "Every proper jail has bars. But we'll fix 'em." And he did. Now the frames, bars and all, swung out like a casement window. All you had to do was to push them and climb out.

"We didn't have time, after we heard his voice," Freddy said. "Anyway, it was a good time to have a showdown."

The sheriff shook his head. "He means that about shooting."

"Yes," said Freddy. "He does. Oh dear, I wish I was braver. It just makes my tail come uncurled when I think of it."

The sheriff said consolingly: "I'm sure it would mine if I had one. Confidentially, I'm not very brave myself. What you doing to do?"

"Have a talk with Billy. He really is brave, that boy. Maybe he can think of something. I certainly can't. When I get scared I don't seem to have any thoughts at all."

Chapter 16

Billy didn't have many thoughts either. Freddy had to walk back to the corner where he had left Cy, and then they rode up to meet the boy. Billy told them of Mrs. Wiggins' escape. He said that he had left his father stamping up and down the living room. "I've never seen him so mad at anyone," Billy said. "He's been talking about an ancestor of ours, Sir Henry Margarine; he fought twenty duels and won all of them. Dad says if you were only of noble blood, he'd send you a challenge. But he says you being a

pig, he couldn't demean himself—excuse me,
Freddy, but that's what he said."

"I'm glad he feels that way," Freddy said. "I
don't want him to demean himself by shooting
bullets into me. Oh, good gracious, can't we talk
about something else?"

Billy could, and did. He was delighted with
his new saddle and clothes and pistols. Freddy
promised to teach him how to use a rope—"if I
don't get shot, that is," he said. They rode up
to Otesaraga Lake, and Freddy showed the boy
Mr. Camphor's estate, where he had been care-
taker one summer. They rode races and prac-
ticed stunts of various kinds, and then sat down
on the shore and talked.

Billy pulled a paper out of his pocket. "Look,
Freddy," he said. "I forgot this. When we were
in your house looking for you, your papers got
knocked all over the floor, and I was picking
them up when Dad let that snake out. I didn't
have time to do anything but just stuff it in my
pocket and run. Then later I read it. I guess I
ought to beg your pardon for reading a private
paper, but I saw it was poetry, and—well, anyway, I read it and thought it was fine. Did you
really write it?"

Freddy saw that it was the missing poem—one of the series on the features, about the eyes. "Oh, that little thing," he said, trying to look modest. "Just something I dashed off; it's of no importance, really."

"Oh, I think it's good," said Billy, and he read it out loud.

The Features, No. 6.

THE EYES.

The eyes are brown or black or blue
Or grey, and of them there are two.
They are arranged beside the nose,
One to each side, which, I suppose
Was done because no other place
Was vacant in the human face.
Without eyes we would fall downstairs,
And constantly bump into chairs,
Our table manners too, I guess,
Would be a pretty awful mess.
How helpfully eyes scan the dish
And watch for bones when eating fish,
Or with a side glance, indirect, eyes
Warn us of grease spots on our neckties.
Then, eyes are used to show our feelings,
In place of yells and sobs and squealings.

For instance, to express surprise,
You raise the lids and pop the eyes;
In showing grief, the lids are dropped,
And tears (if any) gently sopped
Up with a handkerchief—a white one,
(And preferably clean)'s the right one.
The eyes are cleverly equipped
With little lids, which can be flipped
Up in the morning, down at night,
To let in or shut out the light.
We could fill pages with our cries
Of admiration for the eyes;
They're indispensable (see above).
True, eyebrows are well spoken of;
The ears are hard to do without;
The nose is useful too, no doubt;
But eyes! Do not dispense with those!
Abandon ears; give up your nose;
But we most earnestly advise:
Hang on most firmly to your eyes.

"My," said Billy, "I don't see how you do it."

"Do you really like it?" Freddy said. "Personally, I like the nose one best."

"How does that go?" Billy asked.

So Freddy recited it. Then he recited the

one about the ears, and the one about the mouth. Then he recited two poems about spring. Then he recited a long one about how nice it was to be a pig. Then he started to recite . . . "My gracious," he said. "You've gone to sleep! Oh dear!" he sighed. "Just the same," he said to himself. "He's a pretty nice boy. He stayed awake about twice as long as any of my friends ever did."

When they were about to separate that afternoon, Billy wanted Freddy to promise to ride with him again the next day. "We don't hunt any more," he said, "now that the farmers are all mad at my father. Oh, I don't blame them; I see now that we did upset things and interfere with them too much. But it was fun just the same. And it's no fun riding around by yourself. We could have some good games."

"Yes, we could," Freddy said. "But you know all the animals are pretty sore at you. Maybe I think you're all right, but they don't."

"I didn't do a thing but laugh at them," said the boy.

"It wasn't that. You were rude to Mrs. Bean the first day you came to the farm. And you were rude to Mr. Bean too. They won't forgive that easily."

Billy was quiet for a minute, then he said: "I guess . . . well, I didn't mean to be, really. Yes, I guess I was. But would—would you ride with me if they weren't sore?"

Freddy didn't answer directly. He said: "It was your whole attitude, Billy. Towards the Beans, towards all of us. I really think that has changed, but I don't know how much. I don't know if it has changed enough so we could get along with you. What do you think about it?"

Billy looked unhappy. "I don't know either," he said. "I don't feel the same about all of you. I didn't know what you were like. I'd like to—" He broke off and said: "Well, wait a minute. There's one thing I ought to do first. Will you come with me?"

He urged his horse forward and Freddy followed. They rode down through the pasture to the farmhouse. A few of the animals were in the barnyard, but they merely stared; none of them laughed. Billy rode up to the back porch, dismounted, went up the steps and knocked at the door. Mrs. Bean opened it.

"How-how do you do, ma'am," said the boy. "I'm Billy Margarine."

Mrs. Bean didn't help him any. She just nodded.

"Well," said Billy, "I just came to say—I want to apologize for being rude to you the other day. I'm very sorry. I hope you'll forgive me."

"Good grief!" Mrs. Bean said. "Why, young man, I didn't think—"

"Just a minute," said a voice behind her, and Mr. Bean looked out. "H'mp!" he said shortly. "Young Margarine. Yes. Well, boy, what brings you here?"

"Now, Mr. B, just hold your horses," said Mrs. Bean. "Billy came to apologize to me for being rude. Don't bite his head off."

"Yes, sir," said Billy, "and I want to apologize to you, too. I guess Freddy was the one that showed me that—well, that I wasn't very nice."

"Ho! Freddy!" Mr. Bean croaked behind his beard. "Our little boy." He nudged Mrs. Bean with his elbow. Then he frowned. "Well, boy, what did you want to be rude for?"

"Well, I-I guess," Billy stammered—"I guess I didn't know any better."

"Tscha!" said Mr. Bean. "That ain't so. Oh,

now, don't get mad. It ain't so because you do know better or you wouldn't be here."

"Oh, good land, Mr. B," Mrs. Bean exclaimed; "don't badger the boy. He's apologized and that wipes the slate clean. There's a chocolate cake here if Mr. Bean hasn't gobbled it all. Yes, Freddy, you come in too. Cy, I'll send you out a piece; you're too big. Last time we invited a horse into the kitchen he knocked over the range. That was Hank, at Mr. Bean's birthday party last winter."

Half an hour later Billy came out, full of chocolate cake, and climbed on his horse. "My," he said. "They're awful nice people!"

Freddy grinned. "You mean they have awful nice cake."

"No I don't either," said the boy. "And you know I don't. Look, Freddy, how about tomorrow?"

Freddy swung into the saddle. "I'll ride part way with you," he said. "Well, about tomorrow—" He didn't say anything for a short distance. A squirrel was sitting on a fencepost, and he began to giggle when he saw Billy. "Tee-hee!" he said in an affected voice. "O who is that gorgeous young man with our Freddy?" Then two other squirrels joined him and they all giggled and pointed.

Billy turned red, and Freddy thought he was going to get mad. But he didn't. He grinned at the squirrels. "Hi, midgetbrains," he said. "Shake the moths out of your fur."

The squirrels stopped giggling and stared, and Freddy laughed. "I'd like to ride with you tomorrow," he said. "Only I have to keep out of your father's way. How can we manage it?"

Billy said he thought he could find out where his father would be, so they agreed to meet next morning up by the Big Woods, and Freddy turned back home.

But it didn't work. Twice in the next few days—once up by the lake, and once on the Centerboro road—Freddy ran into Mr. Margarine; and both times he had to ride for his life; with pellets from Mr. Margarine's shotgun whistling around his ears. After the second encounter Cy refused to go with him any more. "I'll ride around the farm with you," he said. "Because Old Murderous won't come on the Bean property, but I'm not going to get my hide all full of shot holes."

Both times he had to ride for his life.

Billy wasn't any help either. "Dad won't tell me where he's going to be," he said. "I never saw him so mad about anything—he sure will shoot you if he gets a chance. And I almost think he'd shoot me if he found out I'd been with you."

It got so finally that Freddy didn't dare move off the farm. And at last he made up his mind that something would have to be done. He had a talk with Jacob, the wasp, and then he wrote a note which No. 23 carried over and delivered at the Margarine door. This was what he wrote.

Frederick Bean, Esq., has the honor to challenge Mr. Elihu Margarine to a duel. The terms of the encounter are to be as follows:

WEAPONS: pistols, guns, knives, axes or clubs. Any or all.

TIME: Next Friday evening, eight p. m.

PLACE: All that tract or parcel of pasture land situated between the Big Woods on the northeast and the Margarine buildings on the southwest.

PURPOSE: To shoot Mr. Margarine so full of holes that he will stop bothering me and mind his own business.

p. s. When you ride out of your yard at eight p. m. Friday, come out shooting.

Yours truly,

Freddy.

Freddy wasn't sure that this was the proper form in which to issue a challenge, but he was certain that it would make Mr. Margarine mad enough to come out. And with the arrangements he had made, he felt that he had a pretty good chance of winning, even though his gun was loaded only with blanks. But it had been hard to persuade Cy. "Me," he said—"I'll be just the innocent bystander—the one that always gets the free ride to the hospital."

"Margarine's horse'll be there," Freddy said. "You going to back down in front of that slick snooty thoroughbred!"

This appeal was successful, but Cy begged Freddy to be careful. "Keep a good distance between me and that shotgun, please!" he said. "Those buckshot he uses aren't good for the complexion." Of course Cy knew of the arrangements Freddy had made or he wouldn't, he said, go out in that field Friday night for a whole freight car full of prime oats.

Indeed the scheme was very dangerous. Freddy knew that he stood a good chance of getting killed. "I'm not brave," he said to Mrs. Wiggins. "I'm just desperate. I can't go on living like this, afraid to stir a foot off the farm; I'll lose my self-respect. If he shoots me, Mrs. Wiggins, I'd like you to have all my poems. Maybe when you read them over you'll think of me."

"Oh Freddy don't *talk* like that!" she said, and her big eyes filled with tears.

When Mrs. Wiggins cried, she made almost as much racket as when she laughed. You could hear her for miles. Freddy decided he had better stop her right there. "No, no," he said; "good gracious, I'm not worried, Mrs. W. Frankly, I don't think that Margarine will show up at all Friday night. No sir, I'll live to write dozens more poems to read aloud to you."

Mrs. Wiggins looked at him, and a big sob that was coming up in her throat, turned into a laugh, and she said: "That's what I'm afraid of." And then she went off into a gale of her great roaring laughter.

"Oh, dear," said Freddy. "Now look what I've done!"

Chapter 17

At one minute to eight Friday evening, Freddy
rode down along the edge of the Big Woods and
then turned out into the rough stony pasture
which he had selected as the field on which he
was to fight his duel with Mr. Margarine. It
was beginning to get dark, and there was an
autumn chill in the air. Freddy shivered and
said: "Golly, I wish it was tomorrow morning."

Cy said: "If you ask me, it will be before Margarine shows up. Shucks, Freddy, he's a bank
president; he isn't going to fight a duel with a

pig. Excuse me, but that's what he's going to say."

Freddy said: "You're wrong. That's just the reason why he will show up—because he won't want people to laugh at him and say he was afraid of a pig. You boys all ready up there?" he called.

Jacob, who with his Cousin Izzy was sitting on the brim of Freddy's hat, called down: "You quit worrying about us. We're right with you, kid."

Suddenly Freddy sat up straight and pulled his gun from the holster. He had heard the clink of a horse's shoe against stone. And then out from behind the Margarine barn at a fast trot rode Mr. Margarine. He was perhaps a hundred and fifty yards away.

"Gosh, Freddy," said Cy in a scared voice. "You said he'd have a shotgun. He's got a pistol."

Freddy said through his teeth—which he was holding tight together to keep them from chattering: "That's our good luck. He might get us with a gun; he can't possibly hit us in this light with a pistol. Not if we keep a good distance away."

"Yeah?" said Cy. "And how do we do that? Look." For Mr. Margarine had seen them; he turned his horse and rode at a canter straight at them.

"Got to keep him off!" Freddy muttered. Then he said: "All ready, Jacob." With a sharp buzz the two wasps rose from the hat brim, circled, and headed for Mr. Margarine. Freddy counted slowly to ten, then he raised the pistol and fired.

Mr. Margarine who had been coming on rapidly, ducked at the shot, then reined his horse aside and rode off at an angle. Freddy, of course, had only fired a blank cartridge, but Jacob, who had been circling above Mr. Margarine's head, at the sound of the shot, whizzed past the man's ear. He sounded like a bullet, and a bullet which hadn't missed that ear by more than a sixteenth of an inch.

As Mr. Margarine sheered off he fired quickly twice. Neither shot came anywhere near Freddy, who raised his gun and fired again. And as he did so, Cousin Izzy zipped past Mr. Margarine's other ear.

Mr. Margarine was scared. The pig must be a fine marksman to come so close in a bad light and at nearly a hundred yards. He made no further attempt to get close to Freddy. For the next ten minutes the duelists circled warily, throwing an occasional shot at each other, then when their six-shooters were empty, hurriedly reloading. One lucky shot of Mr. Margarine's went through the cuff of Freddy's right gauntlet. And once when Freddy fired the wasps got their signals mixed and both whizzed past Mr. Margarine's head, one after the other. It sounded as if the bullet, having missed him on the first pass, had turned around and made another try. He couldn't account for it, and it scared him good.

Much to his surprise, Freddy himself wasn't frightened any more. If it hadn't been for Cy he would probably have kept up the fight as long as he had blank cartridges. But Cy wasn't enjoying himself. "Finish him up, Freddy," he said. "Quit fooling around, will you? First thing you know one of those slugs'll come whistling through your gizzard, and then where'll you be?"

"O K," said Freddy. "Jacob," he called. "Next time he starts to reload. Get set." He held his fire.

Mr. Margarine fired, and a second or two later Izzy landed on Freddy's hat brim. "He's only got one cartridge in now," said the wasp. "When he fires again, close in as he reloads." Izzy buzzed off.

So as soon as Mr. Margarine fired again Freddy reined Cy around and said: "All right—let's give it to him!" And Cy dug his hoofs in and drove straight at Mr. Margarine.

Now Mr. Margarine hadn't expected anything like this, and he had been a little slow in starting to reload. Before he had crammed the last cartridge into the cylinder Freddy was within ten yards of him. Bang! went Freddy's pistol. And at the bang Jacob dove. But he didn't whizz past this time. He slammed into Mr. Margarine's cheek and drove his sting in right up to the hilt. With a yell Mr. Margarine threw up his hands and dropped his pistol; and Bang! went Freddy's gun again and Izzy, who had been sitting on Mr. Margarine's collar, walked down inside and stabbed him just below the Adam's apple. And Mr. Margarine yelled again and shouted: "I'm shot!" and fell off his horse.

Freddy dropped from the saddle and picked

up Mr. Margarine's gun. Then pointing both pistols at his enemy, who was rolling on the ground and moaning, he said: "Get up!"

Mr. Margarine stopped rolling, then slowly he sat up and began feeling of his neck. He took his hand away and looked at it. "No blood!" he said wonderingly.

"I didn't want to kill you," Freddy said. "You wouldn't have had a chance if I'd used regular cartridges; I'm a dead shot. I used these special bullets—they sting, but they don't kill. Now get up."

Behind the fences and walls that bounded the pasture dozens of animals had been concealed. They had come to watch the duel. All of Freddy's friends were there, and animals from all the farms and woodlands within twenty miles. Now they all jumped up and ran out on to the field and surrounded Freddy—an enthusiastic crowd who cheered and whacked him on the back. When Mr. Margarine got to his feet, he found himself completely hemmed in by a mob of animals.

Mr. Margarine probably believed what Freddy had told him about his special bullets. But the animals knew better. They knew that Mr.

Margarine had yelled: "I'm shot," and fallen out of the saddle, because a wasp had stung him. And all at once they began to laugh.

That was the most enormous laughter ever heard anywhere. There must have been more than a hundred animals, large ones and small ones—cows, sheep, horses, cats, dogs, mice, woodchucks—even a couple of opossums who were on their way back from a summer vacation in the Adirondacks. The big ones roared and bellowed, the littles ones squeaked and squealed. Mrs. Wogus got the hiccups, and Hank thoughtlessly whacked a woodchuck on the back and knocked him cold. They had to carry him off to one side and throw water in his face to bring him to.

Mr. Margarine stared around hopelessly. It must have been pretty terrifying, standing there in the dusk, and wherever he turned were the open jaws of dozens of grinning animals. He tried to say something, he tried to glower angrily at them—but it wouldn't work. He had been scared and made a fool of, and worst of all—by a pig. He looked around once more, and then he just couldn't take it. He fell face down on the ground and covered his ears with his hands.

It was then that Mr. Bean appeared. He had heard the shots and the shouting and thought he had better see what was going on. The animals fell back respectfully and stopped laughing. Even Mrs. Wiggins stopped. He took in the scene without showing any surprise—which was not unusual, as nobody could ever see what expression he had on behind those whiskers.

"You better go home, animals," he said. He spoke quietly, but just as quietly the crowd melted away. Only Freddy and Cy stayed.

Mr. Bean bent and took Mr. Margarine by the arm. "They've gone," he said. "You'd better get up."

Mr. Margarine uncovered his ears, then sat up, looked around, and got to his feet. He looked dazed as he walked slowly over to his horse and stood leaning with one arm over the saddle.

"Sorry those animals were trespassing on your land," said Mr. Bean. "'Twon't happen again."

Mr. Margarine waved the apology away weakly. "No matter," he said dully. "Let 'em come. Often's they want to. I'm through. Can't fight 'em." He put his left foot in the stirrup, but Mr.

He just couldn't take it and fell face down.

Bean had to help him to mount. When he was in the saddle he looked down. "That barn," he said. "Keep it red. My wife—just have to get used to it." He rode slowly down towards his house.

Mr. Bean looked at Freddy and slowly shook his head. "Not askin' how you did it," he said. "Don't want to know. Made a public monkey of him, I expect. That's the one thing that kind can't stand. Anyhow—no more trouble from him. I know him. Paint the barn red white and blue, he won't say a word." He put his hand for a minute on Freddy's shoulder. Then he turned and walked off towards home.

The only animal who had not witnessed the duel was Arthur. Everybody now, he was sure, knew that Mrs. Margarine's name for him was Sweetie Pie, and he felt that he just couldn't face them. He sat on the porch of the Grimby house and brooded.

When the sound of the tremendous laughter had rolled up through the Big Woods he had groaned aloud: "They're telling everybody," he said. "They're all down there laughing at me now."

As night came down over the Big Woods his

gloom grew deeper and deeper. "Wretched creature that I am," he said—he always spoke in
highflown language, even to himself—"alas,
what is left for me but to move on again, to
move on to exile in some foreign land, far from
family and friends." He didn't have any family
of course; he just put that in to make the sen-
tence sound better.

So he was sitting there bemoaning his fate,
when there was a rustling in the grass and then
the Horribles appeared. They trooped up on
the porch and formed a circle about him.
Arthur groaned. "And this, this is to be my
farewell to the happy life of Bean—to be reviled
by rabbits!"

The Horribles had begun their dance, but
Arthur began to perk up when he heard what
they were singing.

We are the Horrible Thirty,
We may be bloodthirsty and dirty,
But we know how to stick by a friend.
With our knives we will swear to defend
From ridicule, gossip and laughter
Arthur the cat. And hereafter
If anyone dares mention pie

In his presence, that party will die
With loud howls and most horrible yelpings
As he's chopped into just thirty helpings
Of enemy hash. So beware!
Don't get in the Horribles' hair.
By spreading the tale any farther.
With our lives we'll protect our friend Arthur.

As they went on, Arthur sat up and smoothed his whiskers with one paw. "True friends," he thought—"true friends are the best. True friends," he said to himself poetically. "Are more than great pitchers of cream!

"Just the same," he said to himself after a moment, "Freddy never wrote that chant for them. Freddy would never be guilty of rhyming 'farther' and 'Arthur.'"

The Horribles stopped their war dance and sat down, and No. 23 stepped out in front of them. "Brother Horribles," he said; "gaze upon our friend, Arthur. Are we prepared to defend his honor with our lives?"

"We are, Your Dreadfulness," said the Horribles.

"If anyone dares so much as to mention any kind of pie—apple, mince, peach, apricot—even the lowly squash pie—will we scare him into the jiggles, the squealing squirms, and the Horrible scrabblings (which last is the worst of all fits)?"

"We will, Your Dreadfulness," they replied.

So No. 23 bowed to Arthur and said: "Well then, would your honor care to accompany us down to the farm, where a festival of general rejoicing is now in progress?"

"Very happy to," said Arthur getting up. "I see now that my fears were groundless. You are indeed my friends." And they all marched off down to the farm.

The party that night, celebrating the final defeat of Mr. Margarine, was one of the noisiest ever held on the Bean farm. Everybody was there. Charles was the only one that was late. He had been told about it, of course, but sitting up in his spruce tree, he had got so interested in preparing a lecture which was to be called *I was a Fugitive from Justice,* that he didn't start down to the farm until nearly nine. He made up for that later, however, by doing a very graceful exhibition waltz with Henrietta.

Usually Mr. Bean came out at nine-thirty and sent them off to bed. But that night he didn't come out till midnight, and even then he didn't send them to bed. He sat on a box, smoking his pipe, and watching the dancing, for nearly an hour; and when he went in finally, he only said: "Don't keep it up too late." From Mr. Bean, that was equal to telling them to keep it up all night.

They got to bed at two. And at seven somebody banged on the pig pen door.

It was no good pulling the covers over his head; they just kept on banging. At last he got up, but before going to the door, he looked out of the window to see who was there. And he got the surprise of his life. It was Cy banging on the door with his hoof. But behind him on their tall sleek horses were Billy and Mrs. Margarine, and both of them had on cowboy outfits, and Mrs. Margarine even had a gun belt around her waist, and in it were two of the largest revolvers Freddy had ever seen. As Freddy looked, she pulled one of them out. "This'll get the old hoss thief out of the hay," she said, and fired two shots into the air.

"Golly-O-golly!" said Freddy. "Be right with you," he shouted, and grabbed for his thunder and lightning shirt.

"Good morning," they said when he came

out; and Billy said: "Mother's got something for you, Freddy."

Mrs. Margarine got down from the saddle. She took the pistol she had just fired by the barrel and handed it to Freddy. "This is for you," she said. "In recognition of great services rendered the Margarine family."

Freddy took the gun. "Why that's wonderful," he said. "But I don't—I haven't done anything for—"

Mrs. Margarine held up her hand to stop him. "Let's just say that instead of driving us away, as I think you could have done, you helped us to live here in peace. Mr. Bean is our neighbor now, not our enemy. Are you staying here, Billy? I want to go down and see Mrs. Wiggins." And she mounted and rode off.

"I don't get it," said Freddy. "I just defended myself."

"Mother never did like fox hunting," Billy said. "She's from Wyoming, you know. I guess Dad had the wrong idea. Maybe he's still got it; but anyway he won't try to run the whole neighborhood any more."

"So that's it!" said Freddy. "How about you, then?"

"I don't want to run things," said the boy. "First place, I can't; second place it wouldn't be any fun if I could."

"O K," said Freddy. His two holsters of course were filled, so he tucked the new gun inside his shirt. "Three-gun Freddy and Injun Bill. Come on, let's lie in wait for the stage-coach." He mounted Cy, and they rode off down the road.

Freddy Books Published By
The Overlook Press

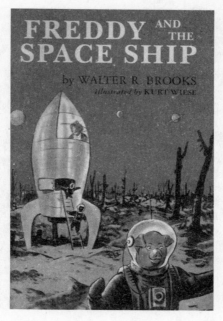

FREDDY AND THE SPACE SHIP
by Walter R. Brooks
ISBN 978-1-59020-469-6 • $10.99 PB

In *Freddy and the Space Ship*, Freddy's homemade rocket is
accidentally knocked off course. A spacepig must be ready
for anything, and Freddy stays calm as he makes an emergency
landing on a distant planet that turns out to be remarkably
similar to the Earth he has left so far behind—a fact which
provides fruitful material for Freddy's philosophizing.

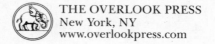

THE OVERLOOK PRESS
New York, NY
www.overlookpress.com

Freddy Books Published By The Overlook Press

THE FREDDY ANNIVERSARY COLLECTION
by Walter R. Brooks
ISBN 978-1-58567-346-9 • $35.00 HC

The Freddy Anniversary Collection contains the first three books in the much-loved Freddy the Pig series, in the order in which they first appeared: *Freddy Goes to Florida* (first published as *To and Again*), along side *Freddy Goes to the North Pole* (*More To and Again*), and the unforgettable *Freddy the Detective*. The collection is perfect for fans and initiates alike: a great starter package and a great collector's edition.

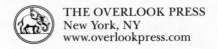

THE OVERLOOK PRESS
New York, NY
www.overlookpress.com

Freddy Books Published By
The Overlook Press

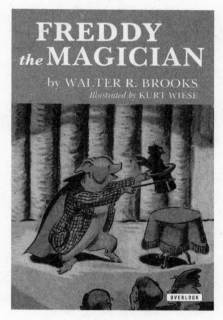

FREDDY THE MAGICIAN
by Walter R. Brooks
ISBN 978-1-59020-481-8 • $10.99 PB

Freddy, who has won so many admirers in his roles of detective,
pied piper, editor, general advisor to the animals on Bean Farm,
and always-poet, will charm readers in his role of magician. Freddy
pulls some wonderful tricks, not the least of which is outwitting
the fraudulent magician who comes to entertain the unsuspecting
inhabitants of the nearby town.

THE OVERLOOK PRESS
New York, NY
www.overlookpress.com

Freddy Books Published By
The Overlook Press

FREDDY AND THE IGNORMUS
by Walter R. Brooks
ISBN 978-1-59020-467-2 • $10.99 PB

Freddy the pig must summon all of his courage and detective skills
when the chief suspect of a series of robberies on Bean Farm is a
legendary beast from the Big Woods.

THE OVERLOOK PRESS
New York, NY
www.overlookpress.com

Freddy Books Published By
The Overlook Press

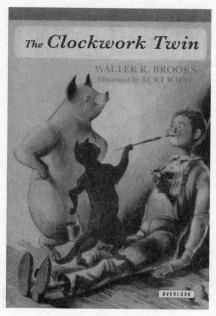

THE CLOCKWORK TWIN
by Walter R. Brooks
ISBN 978-1-4683-0349-0 • $10.99 • PB

In *The Clockwork Twin*, Freddy reprises his most famous role—as detective—when a mechanical double is rigged up by Mr. Bean's brother, Uncle Ben (who is an eccentric inventor), as a friend and playmate for the Beans's adopted boy, Adoniram, a comedy of errors ensues. The Bean farm animals decide to look for Adoniram's real-life brother led by Freddy the detective.

THE OVERLOOK PRESS
New York, NY
www.overlookpress.com

Freddy Books Published By
The Overlook Press

FREDDY AND THE FLYING SAUCER PLANS
by Walter R. Brooks
ISBN 978-1-4683-0319-3 • $10.99 • PB

Freddy the pig is lounging in front of the First Animal Bank when Uncle Ben races by with two sets of flying saucer plans—one true and one false. With spies in full pursuit, he is looking for a safe place to hide the plans—the true ones, of course. As usual, Freddy is ready to help.

A series of hilarious mix-ups ensues, complete with complications provided by Jinx the cat, Mr. J.J. Pomeroy the robin, and the other famous animals from Bean farm. Freddy digs down into his disguises and comes up with a solution to the current problem.

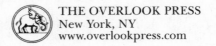

THE OVERLOOK PRESS
New York, NY
www.overlookpress.com

Freddy Books Published By
The Overlook Press

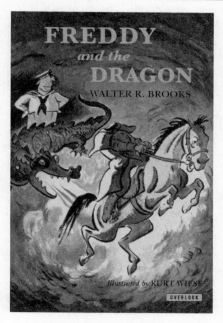

FREDDY AND THE DRAGON
by Walter R. Brooks
ISBN 978-1-59020-866-3 • $10.99 • PB

When Freddy and some of his friends return from a riding trip through
New England, they land right in the middle of a rather cool reception from
the Centerboro citizens. Trouble was afoot and terrible things had been
going on—gardens raided, houses broken into, and even more alarming,
there were threatening notes demanding protection money. Freddy and his
friends set out to solve the mystery, taking on a headless horseman, who
proves no match for Freddy's own dragon!

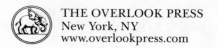

THE OVERLOOK PRESS
New York, NY
www.overlookpress.com

Freddy Books Published By
The Overlook Press

FREDDY AND THE PERILOUS ADVENTURE
by Walter R. Brooks
ISBN 978-1-59020-742-0 • $10.99 • PB

Strange and exciting adventures await Emma and Alice, the two friendly ducks, when they accept Freddy's invitation to ride in a balloon at the Fourth of July celebration. Emma isn't sure she would enjoy it, but Freddy reassures her: "That's the funny thing about adventures. I've had my share of them in my time, as you know, and my experience is that you're enjoying them or not, or else you're just scared. And yet there must be something about them that you like, too, or else you wouldn't go on trying to have more. But the nice thing is afterwards . . ."

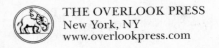

THE OVERLOOK PRESS
New York, NY
www.overlookpress.com

Freddy Books Published By
The Overlook Press

FREDDY THE DETECTIVE
by Walter R. Brooks
ISBN 978-1-59020-418-4 • $10.99 • PB

Freddy is inspired while reading *The Adventures of Sherlock Holmes* to become a detective. Setting out with his intrepid partner Mrs. Wiggins the cow, he is ultimately challenged to prove that Jinx the cat was framed for murder.

FREDDY THE POLITICIAN
by Walter R. Brooks
ISBN 978-1-59020-419-1 • $9.99 • PB

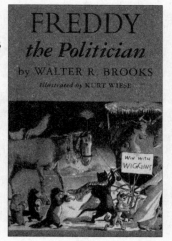

Freddy, the good-natured pig with a poetic soul, is promoting a campaign to get Mrs. Wiggins the cow elected president of the First Animal Republic. As he himself is an officer in the newly organized First Animal Bank, he has more than a modicum of influence— if he can just figure out how to use it.

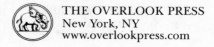

THE OVERLOOK PRESS
New York, NY
www.overlookpress.com

Freddy Books Published By
The Overlook Press

FREDDY AND THE BEAN HOME NEWS
by Walter R. Brooks
ISBN 978-1-59020-420-7 • $9.99 • PB

-:::-

When Freddy's friend Mr. Dimsey is ousted for publishing news of Bean Farm in the local newspaper, the animals decide to take action and publish the first animal newspaper *The Bean Home News*—with Freddy as editor-in-chief, of course! But everyone's favorite pig discovers that being a newspaperman isn't as easy as it looks!

FREDDY AND THE POPINJAY
by Walter R. Brooks
ISBN 978-1-59020-469-6 • $10.99 • PB

-:::-

A robin with poor eyesight has mistaken Freddy the pig's tail for a worm. Putting aside the poem he is writing, Freddy decides to help the poor bird solve his problem. But the solution just seems to lead to bigger problems.

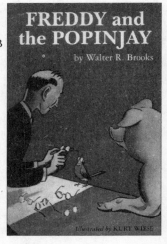

THE OVERLOOK PRESS
New York, NY
www.overlookpress.com

Freddy Books Published By
The Overlook Press

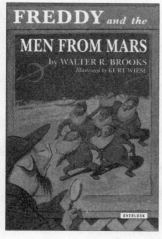

FREDDY AND THE
MEN FROM MARS
by Walter R. Brooks
ISBN 978-1-59020-695-9 • $10.99 • PB

The trouble all starts with the newspaper report that six little creatures, believed to be Martians, have been singlehandedly captured by Herbert Garble. Freddy, ever ready to maintain his reputation as a detective, immediately suspects a hoax, and sets out to expose it. How he does so makes for one of the most hilarious of all Freddy tales.

FREDDY AND THE
BASEBALL TEAM FROM MARS
by Walter R. Brooks
ISBN 978-1-59020-696-6 • $10.99 • PB

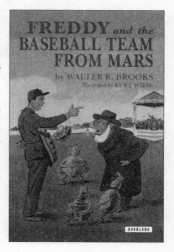

Mr. Boorschmidt's circus in Centerboro boasted a new attraction—six real Martians. Freddy decided to help—by organizing a Martian baseball team. Anyone who can imagine a baseball team consisting of Martians, an elephant, and ostrich, with Freddy as coach, has a slight idea of what's in store.

THE OVERLOOK PRESS
New York, NY
www.overlookpress.com

Freddy Books Published By
The Overlook Press

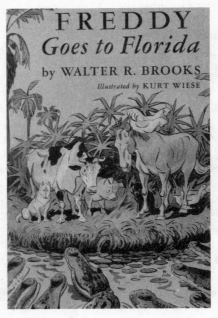

FREDDY GOES TO FLORIDA
by Walter R. Brooks
ISBN 978-1-59020-741-3 • $10.99 • PB

Walter R. Brooks introduced Freddy the Pig in *Freddy Goes to Florida*. Freddy and his friends from Bean Farm migrate south for the winter, with every mile of the way a terrific adventure complete with bumbling robbers and a nasty bunch of alligators. This is vintage Freddy and the whole ensemble cast at their charming best.

THE OVERLOOK PRESS
New York, NY
www.overlookpress.com